She awkwardly [...] her shoulder.

The baby snuggled up next to her neck like his brother had. She shut her eyes for a moment. Casey paused, watching her. There was something in her expression—more than discomfort…pain.

"No pressure, if you'd rather not," Casey said. "It would just help me out, is all."

"I thought you didn't like me," she said, her eyes opening again, and she fixed him with a direct look that made him shift uncomfortably.

"I don't like what you stand for, Ember Reed, but Will seems to settle right down when you're holding him, and babies are like dogs that way. They smell bad people. And like I said, I'm a bit desperate right now. You help me with the boys, and I'll go out of my way to help you find the information you need to make your choice about buying this place. Fair is fair. I'm as good as my word."

Patricia Johns writes from Alberta, Canada. She has her Hon. BA in English literature and currently writes for Harlequin's Love Inspired and Heartwarming lines. You can find her at patriciajohnsromance.com.

Books by Patricia Johns

Love Inspired

Montana Twins
Her Cowboy's Twin Blessings

Comfort Creek Lawmen
Deputy Daddy
The Lawman's Runaway Bride
The Deputy's Unexpected Family

His Unexpected Family
The Rancher's City Girl
A Firefighter's Promise
The Lawman's Surprise Family

Harlequin Heartwarming

A Baxter's Redemption
The Runaway Bride
A Boy's Christmas Wish

Visit the Author Profile page at Harlequin.com for more titles.

Her Cowboy's Twin Blessings

Patricia Johns

Recycling programs
for this product may
not exist in your area.

 LOVE INSPIRED BOOKS

ISBN-13: 978-1-335-47892-4

Her Cowboy's Twin Blessings

www.Harlequin.com

Printed in U.S.A.

And it came to pass, when the people heard the sound of the trumpet, and the people shouted with a great shout, that the wall fell down flat... and they took the city.
—*Joshua* 6:20

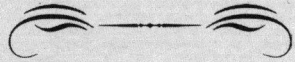

Chapter One

Casey Courtright crossed his arms and chewed the side of his cheek as he looked down at the sleeping newborns. They were in matching cradles in the middle of the sitting room. He felt a wash of tenderness as he watched those little chests rise and fall. He'd had the infants in his house for a week now, and they were growing fast—as was Casey's attachment to them. When he'd agreed to be his cousin's babies' guardian, he'd never suspected to be called upon to take custody! A tragic house fire changed all that… But even with these precious additions to his household, he was pretty sure he could keep his life on track. He had plans—rather immediate ones, actually.

Casey shot the old ranch hand a grateful smile. "I appreciate the babysitting, Bert. My niece should be here to take over in an hour. I've got the bottles ready in the fridge. Diapers are here." He nudged a box with his boot. "Wyatt there tends to wake up first. If you feed him real quick, you can be ready for when Will wakes up. It's a handful with two."

"Sir, I'll be fine," Bert replied, rubbing a hand over

the coarse stubble on his chin. "My wife and I raised five of our own, and we're on our eighth grandchild. Granted, twins'll be a new one for me, but I'm pretty sure I can figure it out for an hour."

"All right, then. Thanks. I'll see you."

If only Casey felt that sure of himself with those two babies. He glanced over his shoulder once more as he headed through the kitchen to the side door. He'd worked here at Vern Acres Ranch for the last fifteen years, ever since his father was forced to sell the family spread. There wasn't much money left over from that sale after debts were paid, and Casey had gone looking for ranching work on someone else's land. That brought him here—Vern Acres. Mr. Vern ran a tight ship, and Casey had climbed in the ranks, finally landing as ranch manager. It was a respected position, but Casey would never feel quite settled until he had his own land again.

Last Sunday in church, the pastor had talked about circling those Jericho walls. God said to march, and they just kept on marching—but seven days of circling those massive, impenetrable walls was a long time. Well, Casey had been circling these walls for fifteen years, looking for an opening, and just before those babies arrived, Casey had seen the cracks start.

Mr. Vern was selling the ranch, and Casey had a down payment saved up and had arranged for a mortgage just large enough to cover what this land was worth. Not a penny more, mind you, but Casey was a man of faith, and he didn't think he'd need that extra penny. He'd been praying for this chance ever since the Courtright land went to Reed Land Holdings, and when he told his dad that he had a chance at getting this ranch, old Frank Courtright had added his prayers to the effort. This morning, Casey was going on up to the main house to tender his offer to Mr. Vern himself.

The drive from the manager's house, where Casey lived, up to the main house took only about five minutes, and Casey's truck bumped over the gravel road in a cheerful rhythm. Spring had come to this corner of Montana. Everything had sprouted—from the grass in the ditches lining to the road to the pasture, lush with tender new growth. Golden sunlight shone through the windshield and warmed up the cab.

This was it—this was the day! And the bright sunlight sparkling off the last of the morning frost on those long, nodding grasses felt like a gift from above. He'd tell the boys about this day when they were old enough to understand—the day the Courtrights got land again. He'd have a ranch to leave to those kids, and they'd be raised right with horseback riding, chores and a personal pride in the land under their feet. And if he could find the right woman, maybe he could even give them a mom.

Casey crested a hill, and the main house came into view. It was a low, wide ranch house with a porch that curved around the side. The backyard was fenced off, with a garden and a shade tree. And beyond the house in the distance, the snowcapped Rocky Mountains loomed in all their glory.

Casey pulled his truck up next to the boss's and turned off the engine. He sat for a moment, raising his heart to his Maker.

Bless this, Lord, he prayed. *This land would be the world to me, if You saw fit to give this Your blessing.*

Then he pushed open the door and hopped out. No time like the present.

The side screen door was propped open with a brick, and Casey could hear the sound of voices as he approached. Mr. Vern's laugh boomed out, and then Casey heard another laugh—softer, more musical. Was a woman in there?

Casey knocked on the door as a formality, then pushed it open as he always did and stepped inside. His eyes took a moment to adjust to the dimmer light of the kitchen. Mr. Vern stood with his arms crossed over his chest, his belly sticking out in front of him. He had a bristling white mustache that covered his lips so that you never could be sure what that mouth was doing unless he was laughing out loud or bellowing an order across a field.

"Morning, Casey," Mr. Vern said. "Good timing. This here is Ember."

Casey turned to make the introduction, and he was met with a tall, lithe blonde woman—bright blue eyes and a smile turning up the corners of her mouth. She was stunning—skin like cream and her lips shining with the lightest touch of gloss. He shook her hand and her grip was firm and confident.

"Pleasure," Casey said with a smile. "You a friend of the boss?"

"Not exactly," Mr. Vern cut in. "She's considering putting an offer down on my ranch, and I need you to give her a tour of the place."

"An offer—" The words stuck in his throat. "Right. Not a problem."

This was his job, after all. He was ranch manager, and he'd be the one who knew the ins and outs of this place. It just came as a shock to hear he had competition already.

"Her car is out front," Mr. Vern added. "She hit that big pothole just before the turn." Mr. Vern exchanged a look with Casey. No one who knew these roads made that mistake. That pothole formed every winter. "Looks like a bent axle to me. She's going to be in town for a bit while she gets that fixed. The tow truck is on its way."

"Great." Obviously, this wasn't the time for Casey's business with Mr. Vern, and already he could feel his opportunity slipping away. Of course, Mr. Vern would be cheery about all of this—the sale of this ranch was going to fund his retirement.

"After you give her the tour, I'd like you to give her a ride back into Victory," his boss said, then turned to the young woman. "The land is beautiful. I have a feeling you're going to fall in love with the place."

Casey smiled tightly. "What was your name again?"

"Ember," she said. "Ember Reed."

"Wait—" Casey's heart thudded to a stop and then hammered fast to catch up. "Reed... Not as in Reed Land Holdings?"

Ember's cheeks flushed. "Yes, actually. But I'm not acquiring land for my father's business. This is a personal purchase."

"Right." As if that even mattered. That wealthy family was the money behind the faceless corporate giant that had been gobbling up the land in the county for years. "Sir, could I have a word?"

Mr. Vern's smile faltered. "Sure. Ember, why don't you go on outside and check out the view. Casey will be right with you."

Ember hitched a purse up onto her shoulder and

headed out the side door. The screen slammed behind her, and Casey watched her look around for a moment before walking away from the door, affording him some privacy. For good measure, Casey swung the door shut.

"Reed Land Holdings," Casey said hollowly.

"I need to sell, Casey. You know that."

"Yeah, but to *them*?" Casey clenched his teeth. "You've seen what they've been doing to this county! We used to be family ranches, shoulder to shoulder, until that soulless giant came through and started buying us out. They own sixty percent of the ranch land out here, and you want to turn that into sixty-five?"

"Linda's care isn't cheap," Mr. Vern replied. "And the place she's in has been going downhill. I need to get her into a better care home."

Mr. Vern's wife, Linda, was suffering from early-onset Alzheimer's, and Casey could sympathize with his boss's sense of urgency here.

"Sir, I was coming up here to make you an offer, myself," Casey said, pulling the folded papers from his pocket. "I've talked to the credit union about a mortgage, and with the money I've saved and the bit that my dad gave me from the sale of his land, I've got enough to make an offer."

"Oh?" Mr. Vern reached for the papers and scanned them. He nodded twice, then shot Casey an apologetic look. "It's a fair offer, Casey. And I appreciate it. If all things were equal, I'd rather sell to you, but Miss Reed says that if she likes what she sees, she can offer twenty percent more than this."

Casey accepted his papers back, emotion closing off his throat.

"I know how this seems," Mr. Vern went on. "I know what your family lost, and I'm not some heartless cad. You know that. But with Linda's cost of care going up, I need every penny I can get. This is my chance to retire, spend what time I can with my wife and set things up for my kids to inherit a little something when my time comes. I'm not young anymore. You might as well know that I'm in a lot of debt. Reed Land Holdings did a number on my profits, too. They've hurt everyone."

"But you're selling to them—"

"I'm *not* selling to them," Mr. Vern retorted. "I'm willing to sell to that young lady out there. Like she said, this a personal purchase for her. Nothing to do with her father at all."

"Funded by him, no doubt," Casey shot back.

"Who am I to judge where someone gets their money?" Mr. Vern shook his head. "Everyone gets it from somewhere, and I don't care if I'm paid by a bank or a checking account. I've got my own worries, Casey. You have to appreciate that. She's not adding this to her father's stash of land—this is for her."

"Her—" Casey hooked a thumb toward the closed door. "That little blonde with the city heels on her boots and the clothes that look like money. She's going to ranch this land herself?"

Mr. Vern shrugged weakly. "Whatever she chooses to do with it is her concern. I've got Linda to worry about, Casey. I'm sorry."

And Casey couldn't argue that point. Mr. Vern loved his wife, and he'd do what he had to in order to get her the care she needed. Casey heaved a sigh.

"I was going to show her around myself, but my old knee is really sore this morning. I need you to show her around," Mr. Vern went on quietly. "I know it's a lot to ask right now, but I also know the kind of man you are. I wouldn't trust this to anyone else, Casey. Besides, she mentioned needing a manager around here. I could make it a stipulation of the sale that you stay employed."

Mr. Vern was trying to help—Casey could see that much—but he didn't have any intention of working for a Reed. Ever.

"I'll do my job, sir," he replied tightly. "You can count on me for that."

He headed for the door. Fifteen years was a long time to work this land, circling those fields and cattle like his own personal Jericho walls. Fifteen years was a long time to pray for God to set things right for his family once again.

It looked like he'd be praying for a little while longer.

Ember turned as the door opened, and that tall, lanky cowboy came back outside. The screen swung slowly shut behind him as he strode into the sunlight and replaced a cowboy hat on his head. He wore a thick vest over his shirt, but his sleeves were rolled up his forearms, revealing solid muscle, and those brown eyes locked on to her somberly—none too glad to see her now that he knew who she was, apparently. He was good-looking in a way she didn't see too often in the city. He wasn't clean-cut by a long shot, but he carried himself with an easygoing confidence.

"Miss Reed, I was asked to show you around," he said. "I'm Casey Courtright, by the way. Ranch manager."

Ember nodded. "Pleasure to meet you. Call me Ember, though."

She turned back to drink in the cattle-dotted hills. It didn't matter which way a person stood on this land, there was a magnificent view from every angle— nothing like her home in Billings. She owned a small apartment in the city—a gift from her father when she graduated with her master's degree in family counseling. And she loved that little apartment. This land, though—this was a chance at something much bigger... Her mark on the world at long last.

She could see a modern silver barn, a web of roads leading away from it. But farther south, there was a red barn, brilliant against an emerald background of pasture, and it kept drawing her eye. If she did buy this land, that barn would stay. She'd have no use for the other one, though.

"You're not a country woman, are you?" Casey said, interrupting her reverie.

"Why do you say that?" she asked, casting him a guarded look.

"Your clothes. Those shoes—" Then he nodded in the direction of the picturesque little barn. "The way you look all wistful when you look at barns."

She smiled, then shook her head. "No, I'm from Billings."

"So what plans do you have for the ranch?" he asked.

"I'm not even sure this is the right ranch," she said, and she noticed the tall cowboy stilled at those words. He raised an eyebrow.

"What do you mean, the right one?" he asked.

"My family had a homestead around here somewhere, and I want to buy the land they used to live on back in the eighteen hundreds."

"Oh." He hooked his thumbs into his belt loops, then shrugged. "And how will you know if you've found the right land?"

"There are some descriptions in old journals. Some names of creeks and rivers… Before I put down an official offer on this place, I need to confirm it's the right property."

"Does Mr. Vern know that?"

"I'm not hiding anything."

From the view that spilled out in front of her, she very well might fall in love with the place as Mr. Vern hoped. But it wasn't the view she was passionate about purchasing, nor would loving the place stop her from walking away. She wanted the land where her ancestors struggled through long winters, where they hunted to keep their growing family fed, where they chopped down trees for their very own log house and barn. Ember's mother had told her stories about the old days when men had to guard their cattle against wolves, and when wagons clattered over trails on their yearly trip to Victory, the closest town they had. Those stories had inspired her, made her feel like she was part of something bigger than herself, something more meaningful.

"You must have people who can look into this stuff for you," Casey said.

"People?" Ember turned to face him. "Oh!" She laughed. "We should probably clear that up right now. Yes, I'm Alistair Reed's daughter, but I'm illegitimate. I don't exactly have the full weight of the Reed legacy behind me. My father helped me get my education and get a start. That's it. I'm not quite the heiress you're taking me for."

"Ah." He eyed her skeptically. "What's your education in?"

"Family counseling." And yes, she noted the irony that she, a dirty little secret for so long, would want to devote her life to helping other families be more functional than hers had been.

"And what do you want the land for?" he asked.

"I want to open a family counseling center—a resort-style environment where families can get away from the pressure of their everyday lives, enjoy some outdoor activities together and talk out their issues." She smiled, wanting him to see and understand her vision.

"So if you bought this place, you wouldn't run the ranch," he clarified.

"No. I'm not a rancher. I'm a therapist."

"Gotcha." Casey chewed the side of his cheek. Was he worried about his own job? Likely. Who wasn't in this current economic climate? She hadn't grown up rich, and she'd only recently come into any kind of money, so she wasn't unfeeling when it came to these issues.

"Casey—may I call you Casey?"

"Might as well," he replied.

"Casey, obviously, I don't even know if I'll buy this place, but if I do, I'll need a manager for the land. I wouldn't be running a full ranching operation, but there'd be horses, some cattle—"

"What would you do with the cattle?" he interjected.

"Do with them?" she said. "Raise them, I suppose. Cattle are very soothing. I think a lot of my clients would benefit with some time in nature."

"So…" Casey squinted. "You'd just feed them? And…keep them?"

"I suppose, yes."

"So your vision is to have fields full of elderly cattle?" He eyed her with a veiled expression on his face, and she was relatively certain he was mocking her.

"I'm not a complete fool," she retorted. "I know where the meat on my plate comes from, but I'm not looking to run a cattle ranch. I suppose those are all decisions I'd have to make later on."

"Fair enough."

"What I was trying to say," she said, "is that if I buy this place, I'll need a manager, and I understand that the prospect of losing a job is a daunting one. You wouldn't need to worry about that."

"I'll land on my feet," he replied tersely. "No need to worry about me."

"Okay." That definitely didn't sound like gratitude for job security. In fact, he sounded like he had no interest in working for her at all. "Is there a reason you don't like me?"

"Let's just say that this county has been hit hard by your father's corporation," he replied.

"My father's corporation provides a lot of good jobs to this county," she shot back.

"Your father's corporation pushed my family out of our ranch," he snapped. "And yeah, the Reed ranches provide jobs—jobs I don't want. I want my land back. But that's not happening, is it? You're an outsider—don't think you know people around here or how we think."

Ember swallowed. "I'm sorry about that. I didn't know."

"Yeah?" He shook his head. "Great. Thanks."

His tone dripped sarcasm, and some anger simmered deep inside. She might not know him or the people around here, but he didn't know a thing about her, either!

"Hey—my mother was the housekeeper in the Reed house," she said. "I wasn't raised in some mansion. My mother gave me the Reed last name on my birth certificate, but my father didn't publicly acknowledge me until I was twenty! We lived in a basement apartment and wore secondhand clothes. My mom worked *hard* in order to provide for us. I'm no spoiled heiress."

"I'm glad to hear it," he replied curtly. "But you're still crossing lines you know nothing about around here. There's such a thing as family pride. We don't want to work for someone else. We want land that's connected to us...land we can pass down."

"And in that, we can finally agree," Ember replied with a tight smile. "I want what you want—land connected to my family. And for the record, the family connection is on my mother's side, not my father's."

Casey met her gaze for a moment. Then his cell phone rang and he dug it out of his front pocket.

"Yeah..." he said, picking up the call and turning away from her.

This ruggedly handsome man didn't like her, but there was more to the anger and frustration he was showing—she could sense it. If he were a client, she'd ask him how all this made him feel. And he likely wouldn't answer. She knew Casey Courtright's type— stubborn, reticent, silent. They were the hardest kind of man to get to open up—the kind that clammed up during appeals to talk inside a therapist's office, but became more relaxed and responsive during outdoor activities like horseback riding or long hikes. Or work.

She eyed Casey as he talked on his phone, his tone low. Yes, Casey Courtright would be the kind of man who valued his work higher than anything else. And she was threatening to change it. Was that his problem with her?

Casey hung up the phone and turned back toward her. "That was one of my ranch hands. He's got to head out to check on a herd, so I need to take over for him." Casey nodded toward his truck. "I can't start the tour until I take care of this, I'm afraid. Care to come along?"

"Take over what?" she asked, her interest piqued.

"Childcare," he replied with a small smile. "I'm the new guardian of twin baby boys, and one of my ranch hands was staying with them, but it looks like he'll have to report back to work."

Baby boys…that hit her right in the heart. She'd had her own baby boy and held him in her arms for one long night, and her memories of him made her heart ache. She sucked in a ragged breath. Casey wasn't the only one to pour himself into his work. She did the same. This trip to discover her family's land was the closest she'd come to anything like a vacation in ages. She was out here until her car was fixed, and she had a mission to discover whether this was the land her family had settled or not. Now was not the time to delve into her own personal issues.

"So you're—" she began.

"Heading back to my place," he said. "It's five minutes down the road." He paused, regarding her with a thoughtful look on his face.

"What?" she asked with a small smile.

"You and I might be able to help each other, Ember. You're obviously going to need some time on this property to figure out if it's the right place. And I need some help with those babies."

"I'm no nanny," she said with a short laugh.

"I'm not asking you to be. I can show you around this ranch properly, but my availability is going to be hit-and-miss. We run a really efficient operation here without a lot of extra employees hanging around, and I'm in a unique situation being a new guardian of these babies. Everything is in a knot right now. Seeing this ranch is going to take you more than one day, and if I'm going to give you a proper tour, I'd need to scrounge up a ranch hand to babysit while I take you around, and I can't always spare the man. My niece helps out, but she's got school and a part-time job of her own, so I can't really count on her. But if you were here on the ranch so you'd be available when I manage to get everything lined up, and if I had some extra help with the babies in the meantime, we could both have our needs met."

"I'm not a long-term solution," she countered.

"I'm not looking for one. My aunt is coming in two weeks to help me out full-time. All I need is a bit of help until then. Plus, your car is in the shop for a week at least, isn't it?"

Ember licked her lips and looked away. He was right—if she was going to get the time on this property that she needed to make an informed purchase, she'd have to make some kind of arrangement to stay. This setup made the most sense. But it didn't take that aching part of her heart into account. Baby boys...she wasn't ready to reopen that wound. Not yet, and not with an audience.

Ember looked back at the house, over at her wrecked car and up into the face of that rugged cowboy. His expression didn't betray any of his feelings, and he raised an eyebrow at her.

"What do you say? You can think about it, if you want. But I've got to head back to the house. Coming or staying?"

This wasn't about old wounds and sad regrets. And she couldn't avoid babies forever. As much as she hated being pushed into a corner like this, she had a priceless opportunity to look at this land with the attention to detail she required. Could she set aside her personal issues long enough to make her dreams for her future work come true? She sucked in a breath, her limited options circling her mind.

"I'm coming," she said.

Somehow, Ember needed a fresh start...and this land held a promise of just that.

Chapter Two

Casey looked over at the woman beside him in the passenger seat as he bumped over that familiar gravel road. She looked relaxed enough, unless he noticed her hands—white knuckled in her lap. Was it him? Was she nervous about driving down some isolated ranch road with a guy she didn't know? He didn't like the idea of anyone being truly afraid of him. She was the competition—here to slap down more money than he had any access to—but she was also a woman out of her element and alone, and that made him soften toward her a little bit.

"You okay?" he asked.

"Of course."

"Because you're white knuckling it there." He shot her a half smile.

"Oh…" She breathed out an uncomfortable laugh. "Sorry."

She released her grip, stretched her fingers out and laid her hands flat against the tops of her legs.

This drive back down the road wasn't quite the celebration the drive up to the house had been. Was this it, then? Mr. Vern would sell to this city slicker, and Casey's dreams of owning a ranch would have to be put on hold yet again? Yes, there was always the chance that another property would land on the market, but would the timing ever be right again? Those babies were going to cost money to raise, and he'd be chipping into that down payment he'd squirreled away in no time. Plus, he knew he couldn't do this alone indefinitely. His aunt would come help full-time for a while, but she'd never take the place of a real mom. He hoped to get married and bring his wife back to his own land…not another man's.

"So how much have you researched about this ranch so far?" Casey asked.

"The maps I could find online and in local records were limited," she replied. "But my great-great-grandmother wrote a journal where she talked about some specific landmarks. If I could find the actual site of the old house, there's something I know to look for. My great-great-great grandfather put a single red brick in the front of the fireplace. It was something they brought from across the country—a touchstone of sorts. I don't know if I'll be able to find it, though. Plus, I'm waiting to hear back from some local historical societies."

Casey glanced toward her again. "And if you don't find the landmarks?"

"I don't have unlimited resources, so this purchase has to be the right one. If this isn't the land I think it is, then I'm not buying it. There are cheaper ways to open therapy centers."

Hope surged up inside of Casey's chest. Maybe Ember Reed was just a temporary inconvenience on the Vern ranch. Maybe this wasn't the spot her family had settled after all, she'd go on her way and he could buy this land fair and square. He had plans for raising a family here, too—an honest, hardworking family who would raise cattle and ranch like the generations of Courtrights before him. Casey knew this ranch like the back of his hand. It wasn't a huge operation, but he'd been running it well, and the chance to be a landowner once more... it was enough to make him hope in that dangerous way that meant his heart was already set on it.

He had an attachment to this land already, too. He'd imagined himself living up in the big house, hiring another manager and being the owner who called the shots...and in his mind, that felt really good! He'd be able to bring his dad back to live with him, and his old man could live his last years on Courtright land.

So, yeah—if it didn't make things harder on Mr. Vern and his sick wife, Casey would like to see this land come to him. He was praying that God would provide for them all.

"That's my place ahead," Casey said as he turned into the drive that led up to the ranch manager's house. It was within sight of the ranch hands' bunkhouse just down another gravel road. The ranch manager's house was a small one-bedroom bungalow, and as he parked and pushed open the truck door, he could already hear the babies' plaintive wails, and he felt that wave of anxiety he always did at the sound of their cries.

Ember hopped out, too, and she followed him around the truck toward the side door of the house. Casey pulled open the door and held it for Ember, letting her step inside ahead of him. Bert stood in the kitchen with

Wyatt in his arms, a bottle in one hand and a panicked look on his face.

"They woke up at the same time, boss," Bert said.

"I'll get Will," Casey said, heading through to the sitting room, and he scooped up the baby, settling him into the crook of his arm. The baby kept up his wailing, and Casey headed back to the kitchen, turning on the hot tap on his way past the sink.

"Ember, would you grab the bottle in the fridge?" he said.

Ember did as he'd asked and handed it over. Casey stuck it under the hot tap until the count of twenty, then shook it up and tested it against his hand. Warm. Perfect. He popped the nipple into Will's mouth, and there was blessed silence as both babies slurped back the milk.

"I'm Bert," the old ranch hand said, nodding to Ember.

"This is Ember Reed," Casey said. "She's—" how much to say? "—she's a special guest of Mr. Vern's. I'm showing her around."

"Pleasure." Bert smiled. "But I've got to head out. I still have work to do out there. Mind if I just pass this little guy over?"

Ember's eyes widened, and she was about to answer when Bert deftly eased the baby into her arms. Bert stood there, still holding the bottle until Ember had the baby in a comfortable position and took the bottle from his hands.

"Thanks, Bert," Casey said. "Much appreciated."

"Yup. Not a problem." Bert took his hat off the top of the fridge, dropped it onto his head and headed out the side door.

Casey looked over at Ember, and he saw a stunned look on her face. She wasn't looking at the baby, even though Wyatt was slurping back that bottle in record time. What was with her? This was a baby, not a hand grenade.

"Bert there is one of the ranch hands," Casey said. "He's worked here for thirty years, and he's good at his job. He's one of the guys who'll be out of work if this isn't a full-scale ranch anymore."

Wyatt finished with his bottle, and Ember put it down on the kitchen table, then took a moment to get the little guy up on her shoulder, patting his back in a slow rhythm. Wyatt snuggled into her neck, and Ember sighed, tipping her cheek against his downy head.

"He likes you," Casey said.

She didn't answer, but she smiled wanly and continued her gentle patting of the baby's back. Then Will finished with his bottle, and Casey popped the nipple out of his mouth and put the infant up onto his shoulder, too.

"I'm not trying to put people out of work," Ember said.

"I'm just pointing out the reality of things," Casey replied. "Mr. Vern asked me to show you around, and I'm going to do that. But I'm not going to sugarcoat anything, either. You'll get a real tour of the place— see what this ranch is, the people whose livelihoods depend on it. You need to understand the whole picture, not just what you could turn this place into if you swept it clean."

"You're one of those guys who doesn't believe in talking about his feelings, aren't you?" she asked with a small smile turning up her lips.

"What have I just been doing?" he asked. "I thought I was pretty clear about my feelings here. I talk. But I generally do it around a campfire on a cattle drive—away from civilization, like a real man."

"And ironically enough, that's the experience I want to provide to men from the city," she said. "Because you're right—sitting in a counselor's office with a tissue box in front of his wife isn't the most inviting atmosphere for a man to open up."

"The real work on a cattle drive makes a difference in how much we'll open up, too, you know," he said. "Responsibility, exhaustion, pushing yourself to the limit. You can't simulate that in some counseling setting with a bonfire."

Casey's cell phone rang, and Casey had to adjust the infant in the crook of his arm as he dug the handset out of his pocket. He glanced at the number—it was his niece who was supposed to arrive any minute, and his heart sank. No one called at the last minute to say there was no problem... Will squirmed and Casey rocked him back and forth as he hit the talk button.

"Hi, Nicole," Casey said, after picking up. "Where are you?"

"I'm sick, Uncle Casey..." Yep, exactly what he'd been scared to hear. "I think it's the flu. I'm so sorry."

He sighed. "It's okay, kiddo." He glanced over at Ember once more. Had she made her decision yet about sticking around for a little while? "Don't even worry about it. Feel better, okay?" After a goodbye, he hung up the call.

Ember's phone rang just then, and he sighed. He'd have to wait to get an answer from her. As she talked in low tones, Casey looked down into Will's tiny face.

"You're wet, aren't you, little guy?" he murmured. The babies were always wet after a bottle—it was one of those constants he could depend upon. He glanced over at Ember, and she stood there with the baby up on her shoulder, her gaze directed down at the floor as she listened to whoever was on the other line.

Casey kicked the new diaper box across the kitchen floor toward the living room. This was the routine. He kept a towel laid out on the couch, and he'd been using that as a changing station. It was a rough setup, but it seemed to work out okay.

He laid Will on the couch cushion and sat on the couch next to him to do the honors.

"That was the mechanic," Ember said, coming into the room.

"Oh, yeah?" Casey set to work on the sodden diaper, then reached for a new one. He was getting pretty good at this, but two babies went through a phenomenal number of diapers a day. He rolled up the soiled diaper, then lifted the little legs to pop a new one underneath the baby's tiny rump.

"It'll be over a week before my car will be fixed," she said. "There are other cars ahead of mine, and—" She sucked in a breath. "How would it work if I stayed on this ranch for a few days?"

"I'd talk to Mr. Vern, explain the situation and see if he'd be okay with you staying up at the big house," Casey said. "You wouldn't have to worry about inappropriately close quarters here at my place, but you'd be close enough to make everything relatively convenient. I can pick you up and bring you back here no problem."

He fiddled with the snaps on Will's sleeper—they

were so easy to accidentally snap together one snap off-center so that he'd have to start all over again...

"What about your niece?" she asked.

"She's got the flu, but even if she didn't, the kid's fifteen. She's supposed to be in school, not minding children."

Ember eyed him. "And just to be clear..." She let it hang.

"I just want a hand. I'll find people to babysit when I give you the tours and all that, but I need another person—another set of hands until my aunt can get here. You can see how much work they are. We could both benefit, if you're game. What do you say?"

Ember looked down at the baby in her arms and wrinkled her nose. "This little guy dirtied his diaper."

Casey chuckled. "Let's trade. Will here is clean."

Casey took Wyatt from her arms, and Ember awkwardly lifted Will up onto her shoulder. The baby snuggled up next to her neck like his brother had. She shut her eyes for a moment. Casey paused, watching her. There was something in her expression—more than discomfort...pain.

"No pressure, if you'd rather not," Casey said. "It would just help me out, is all."

"I thought you didn't like me," she said, her eyes opening again, and she fixed him with a direct look that made him shift uncomfortably.

"I don't like Bert, either, but who can be picky?" he said, shooting her a teasing smile. "I'm joking. I don't like what you stand for, Ember Reed, but Will seems to settle right down when you're holding him, and babies are like dogs that way. They smell bad people. And like I said, I'm a bit desperate right now. You help me with the boys, and I'll go out of my way to help you find the information you need to make your choice about buying this place. Fair is fair. I'm as good as my word."

"Okay," she said with a nod.

He felt a wave of relief. At least he'd have a hand here for a few days, and that was a bigger boost to his peace of mind than she seemed to realize. "I'll talk to Mr. Vern, then."

She smiled wanly. "I'm not good with kids—the childcare side, I mean. I should at least warn you."

"It's just diapers and bottles," Casey said, grabbing another fresh diaper and the bucket of wipes. "I only started on this a week ago, and I've gotten pretty good at it. You'll catch on."

And here was hoping that when he'd done his duty and shown her the ranch, she'd decide not to buy the place. But that was in God's hands—the hardest place to leave it.

When Casey was finished with the diaper, they traded babies again. She was getting better at this—easing one baby into his arms and taking the other baby into her own. Ember looked down at the tiny boy in her arms. Wyatt. The baby was wide-awake, those deep brown eyes searching in that cross-eyed, newborn kind of way. She lifted him closer to her face, inhaling the soft scent of his wispy hair.

She'd held her own newborn son in her arms ten years ago, and she'd breathed in the scent of him. She hadn't named him. That wasn't her role, but she knew the name the adoptive family had chosen—Steven. She would always remember how he'd felt in her arms, how her heart had stilled just having him so close…

After spending one tearful night cradling him, feeding him with a bottle of formula lest she grow too attached, she'd passed him over to his new mom and her heart had broken. The sound of his cry as they took him away had slid so deep into her soul that she dreamed of it at night even now, and woke up with achingly empty arms.

It had been for the best—that was what she told herself. But she wasn't so sure anymore. Ember sucked in a stabilizing breath.

"How did you end up with these babies?" she asked.

"My cousin and his wife had asked me to be their guardian should anything happen," Casey said. "I thought it was nothing more than a gesture, because I'm single. I'm a ranch manager. I don't have time for kids, right? But then there was this horrible fire, and they managed to get the boys out, but Neil and Sandra didn't make it. That left the kids with me." He cleared his throat, blinked a couple of times.

"Will you keep them?" Ember asked hesitantly.

"Keep them?" Casey repeated, casting her a questioning look. "Yeah, of course. I'm the closest family they've got. What else would I do?"

"Some might let them be adopted by another family," she said.

"Yeah, some might." Casey finished with the sleeper's snaps, noticed he'd done them up wrong and whipped them all open again to start fresh. "And honestly, it did occur to me. But—I don't know. I can't bring myself to do it."

Ember nodded. She'd felt nearly the same way…but she hadn't seen any other choice. She remembered how helpless she'd felt at the prospect of single motherhood

and losing the support her father offered if she didn't cooperate and give the baby up…

"How will you do this?" Ember asked. "Raise them on your own, I mean."

"How does any parent raise their kids?" Casey picked up the baby and put him onto his shoulder, then headed through to the kitchen. The water turned on, and he raised his voice to be heard. "I figure I'll just wing it. Isn't that what the rest do?"

Ember chuckled at that. "I'm more of a planner, myself."

"Well, I've got a few plans," Casey said, coming back into the room as he awkwardly dried his hands on a paper towel while balancing the baby on his shoulder. "My aunt has agreed to watch the kids for me during the days. I'll pay her, of course. And I've been advised by a nice lady in social services that I should have them sleep on their backs without blankets, and that I should be feeding them once every three hours." He lifted his watch on his wrist. "And counting, right?"

He was strangely optimistic, this cowboy, and she regarded him in silence for a moment.

"Now, I've got some maps of this land," Casey said. "I don't know if it's anything you haven't seen yet—"

"That would be great," Ember said. "You never know."

Casey turned away from her and headed for a cupboard in the corner. He opened the door with a squeak, and a roll of paper fell out. He used the toe of his boot to lift it, and grabbed it with his free hand. He passed it back toward her. "That might be one. Hold on…"

He rummaged a bit, handed back three more rolls

of paper, then closed the cupboard and readjusted the baby on his shoulder again.

"Will, you're going to have to sit in that little chair of yours."

Ember watched as Casey pulled out a wire-framed bouncy chair from beside the couch, then arranged the baby in it. Little Will turned his head to the side and stared at a patch of sunlight on the wall. Then Casey pulled out a second bouncy chair, and relief welled up inside her at the thought of putting Wyatt down.

She was already dreading this—the baby minding. These tiny boys brought up feelings she wasn't ready to deal with. Or rather, feelings she'd been trying to deal with rather unsuccessfully. It was supposed to get easier over time—that was what they said—but it hadn't.

"Here we go, Wyatt," she murmured, bending to put the baby into the chair next to his brother, but as she tried to put him down, Wyatt's little face screwed up into a look of displeasure and he opened his mouth in a plaintive wail.

"Or not." She stood back up and the crying stopped. She looked into Wyatt's little face, and he peered back at her. "You sure?"

"Guess he likes you, too," Casey said. "Never mind. I'll open these up."

Ember's heart sped up as she looked from the baby to his guardian, and then back again. This was not a good plan, but what was she going to do? She'd already agreed to this, and if she backed out, she'd only cement her reputation as the heartless city girl who'd come to ruin everyone's lives.

Casey opened one of the rolls and revealed a map. "So what are you looking for, exactly?"

"The journal mentions Milk River and some creeks that ran off it."

"Milk River runs for over seven hundred miles," he said, glancing back at her. "We only have about fifty miles of Milk River on this ranch."

She nodded. "I think it might be the right fifty, though. The creeks were named after local wildlife— Beaver Creek, Muskrat Creek and Goose Creek."

Casey looked closer, chewing on the side of his cheek. "This here is Milk River." He pointed with one calloused finger, following a line along the map. "There are a couple of creeks, but they're not named. Not officially." He rerolled the map, then picked up another one. He scanned it, rolled it up again and picked up the third. "Here we go. That's Milk River again—"

Ember leaned closer to look. The line of the river meandered down the map, and there were about fifteen little lines snaking off. The darker of the lines had names, and cocking her head to one side, she could read them.

"Allan Creek. Wallace Creek. Burns Creek. Trot's Creek…" She sighed. Then there were the lighter lines that had no names. She'd seen this map already online. Back in the city, she'd been looking for mention of the Beaver, Muskrat and Goose creeks, but no one seemed to have record of them. Maybe those names hadn't stuck.

"Milk River goes up into Canada, you know," he said. "I don't have the maps for that."

Then her eye landed on one creek name she hadn't seen before that brought a hopeful smile to her lips. "Look at that one!" She pointed. "Harper Creek!"

"That's familiar?" Casey asked with a frown.

"My mother's last name was Harper. That's the family name."

"Hmm." He nodded. "Okay."

"What's the matter?" Wyatt was getting heavy in her arm, and she shifted him to a new position.

"There are a lot of Harpers around here," he said. "They might be relatives of yours, though."

She'd never heard of them, if they were. It might be nothing more than a coincidence. Or a creek named much more recently—a random moniker slapped onto a tiny creek in honor of some locals.

"We aren't Canadian. My mother always said that the family had settled exactly fifty miles from the mountains, and they'd been another forty miles from Victory. That's right here. This land. Give or take."

Casey nodded slowly. "Approximately, yes."

"I know it's a very rough estimate, but since this land came up for sale, I wanted to check it out," she said.

"Well, we'll have a look," Casey said, but his expression was grim.

"You don't want me to buy this land, I know," she said.

"You're right," he agreed. "I don't. This is prime ranching land, and cattle fuel this community. It's our way of life, and I've worked this herd for fifteen years now. There's something to be said for consistency. Also, there's honor in feeding America's families, and the beef we raise is top quality. That matters to me. To see this place turn into some therapy center— No offense, ma'am, but from my way of thinking, it would be a crying shame. The city folk might need their therapy and their chance to enjoy the wide outdoors, but we ranchers need pasture under our boots and cattle to drive. So what you're suggesting isn't going to help us at all. Again, no offense."

"None taken," she murmured.

"But that doesn't mean I won't treat you honestly," Casey said.

"Can I be sure of that?" she asked.

"I'm a rancher, Miss Reed," Casey said, his voice a low growl. "But I'm also a Christian. That one sits a little heavier. I believe in right and wrong, and I stand with the truth. So if I find out that this is the land you've been looking for, then I'll tell you honestly, because I want God's blessing more than I want my way. And God's never yet blessed a lie."

Ember regarded him thoughtfully.

"Are you a Christian, Miss Reed?" he asked.

"Yes," she said.

"Then a handshake should be enough, wouldn't you say?" he asked, holding out one hand toward her.

Ember took his rough hand in hers, and she felt the gentle pressure of those strong fingers. It was a muscular hand—veined and broad—and she realized anew just how attractive this stubborn cowboy was. She tugged her fingers free.

"Could you take the baby back?" she asked, slightly breathlessly.

Casey did as she asked and she slid the infant into Casey's arms. Wyatt didn't complain this time, and she exhaled a shaky sigh.

This was the right land—she could feel it. Everything had fallen into place in that way that God had where she could sense His fingerprints on all of it. From the sale of the swampland, down to this ranch popping up for sale just at the same time she'd pinpointed an approximate location of the Harper homestead.

Ember had felt drawn here, but looking at that lanky cowboy and the babies he was honor bound to care for, she couldn't help but wonder if this was God's doing for other reasons entirely—like forcing her to face her own issues. Ember wanted to belong somewhere—be someone other than the illegitimate child of a wealthy man. She wanted a connection so solid that her paternity wouldn't be the most defining factor in her lineage any longer.

The sooner she could investigate this land and decide on her next move, the better.

Chapter Three

$Mr.$ Vern, as it turned out, was perfectly happy to have Ember stay with him if she was helping out his ranch manager. Those babies had sunk into his heart, too, it seemed.

"They need loving," Mr. Vern said. "That's all. Just loving. But there's two of them, and Casey's got a big job. So I think we all appreciate you being willing to snuggle some babies. It'll take a village with those boys."

A village was the precise thing she hadn't had on her side when she'd been pregnant with her son. If there'd been a village for her, she might have been able to keep her little boy, but she didn't have any support. When she'd told her father about her pregnancy, he'd recommended an abortion, but said that if she insisted on having the baby, she'd have to give it up for adoption. He wasn't interested in supporting her for the long term. He'd agreed to pay for her education, but his one stipulation to his support had been that she *act like a Reed* and not embarrass the family. Raising a baby on her own without a husband apparently violated that clause. Set aside the fact that she'd been fathered in an affair…but Alistair was the one with the money and she wasn't in a position to argue with him about his morals. It had seemed hopeless then…

Ember lay between crisp sheets that night, listening to the soft sounds of a strange house, and she lifted her heart in prayer. She'd been so sure when she'd come out here—confident, excited. But somehow, she'd gone from completely in control to feeling entirely out of her depth.

Lord, I need Your help, she prayed. *I don't know how I got myself into this, but here I am…*

Only God knew how she'd been struggling with memories of her own son lately. She'd naively thought that giving him up would allow her to move forward with her life. And in some ways, she had, but lately, memories of that traumatic day were coming back like punches to the gut. So she lay in bed *not* asking for God to help her sort out her emotions right now, because she knew better than to ask for that! A woman didn't hop over her feelings; she waded through them. And wading would have to wait until she was finished with this task at hand. As ironic as it was for a therapist, she wanted God to help her put a lid on her feelings. For now, at least.

Ember slept remarkably well that night. Maybe it was the exhaustion from the adventures of her day, but she didn't even stir until she awoke to the distant aroma of brewing coffee. Ember rubbed a hand over her face and reached for her watch, checking the time. It was just after six, and outside, the sky was awash in pink. She pushed back the covers and reached for her clothes. She'd come with a bag packed and had intended to stay

in a local hotel for a few days, so she had a few necessities with her. Ten minutes later, she'd washed up, put on a little makeup and made herself presentable before leaving the bedroom for the kitchen.

Mr. Vern stood in front of the stove, a bowl of whisked eggs in one hand as he flung a pat of butter into a sizzling pan.

"Good morning," he said without turning.

"Good morning." She headed for the coffeepot. There were two mugs waiting, and she filled one. "Is this for me?"

"Sure is," Mr. Vern said. "I'm just whipping up some eggs now, too."

"You're up early," she said.

"I've already been out to check on some cattle," he said with a low laugh. "I saw Casey down there, and he said to tell you that he's got a ride planned toward Milk River today. He thought you might be interested."

"Oh!" Ember brightened. "Yes, I am."

"He says he's planning on leaving about seven," Mr. Vern said. "You'll want to eat hearty before then. Have you ridden before?"

"No," she confessed.

"Hmm." Mr. Vern glanced back at her, a look in his eye like he was sizing her up. "It's a good way to take a look at the land, but…"

"I'll be fine," she reassured him. "I'm assuming I'm in good hands with Casey Courtright?"

"The best." Mr. Vern poured the egg mixture into the pan. "In fact, you'd do well to keep him on, Miss Reed. He knows this land better than I do at this point."

"He's already said that he's not interested in working for me," she admitted.

"Has he now?" Ember couldn't see the older man's face, but his tone sounded displeased. "That's just pride. Give him time."

Time for what? She didn't want to be saddled down with an employee who didn't want to be here. But this wasn't the time to discuss that.

After breakfast, Mr. Vern drove her down the sloping gravel road, his radio playing a jangly gospel tune. Mr. Vern wore a dusty trucker's hat, and he chewed on a toothpick as he drove.

"So left, we've got the cattle barns—you can see them, right? The big modern silver ones. Those are used for some calving, injured animals and the like. For the most part, the cattle spend their days in the field. I'll bring you down there later if Casey hasn't got the time."

The older man followed the road right, heading away from the cattle barns and toward that picturesque red barn bathed in golden morning sunlight.

"There's four hundred acres in total—that includes the forest as well as the pasture. I know you're not interested in raising cattle, but the property includes about two hundred head that we've raised for market. So you'd have at least one market run. Casey would be able to fill you in on the finer details there, of course."

"Where are we going?" Ember asked.

"To the horse barn," Mr. Vern said. "We've got twenty-two horses at present. Our ranch hands use them when they check on herds and that sort of thing. Now, there are three horses that belong to Casey personally, and another two that I'm not willing to part with. But the other seventeen are included in the sale."

"Are they good for trail rides?" she asked.

"About five are gentle enough for newbies, but the others need a more experienced hand," he admitted. "I can sell off the others first, if you want. Just to save you the trouble later."

"We'd have to talk about that," she agreed with a nod.

"Some ranches like to use quads for checking the herd, but I've stuck to the tried and true. We've got a paddock, and since you mention trail riding, we've got some good trails, too." They rattled over a pothole, and Mr. Vern shot her a grin. "If you do buy this land, miss, you're going to need a solid truck. I'm a Ford man, myself."

Ember could see the wisdom in those words. Her car had already shown that it would be jolted right apart on some of these roads. But as they crested a hill, her to-do list melted away at the sight.

Green field rolled out beneath them, fence posts running like lines of neat stitches across the verdant plains. Some horses were grazing—one tiny foal trailing close to its mother. The red barn stood out in comforting contrast to the rest of the scene, and Ember felt all that tension seep out of her body. They eased down the road toward the red barn, and as the truck came to a stop out front, a door opened and Casey looked out. He was dressed in a pair of jeans, a button-down shirt and a padded vest. He pushed his cowboy hat back on his head and raised a gloved hand in a wave.

"Have a good day," Mr. Vern said. "If you have any questions, Casey's the one to ask. Like I said, stubborn lout or not, that man is worth keeping around. Mark my words."

Ember thanked him and hopped out of the truck.

Casey waited for her at the door, holding it open for her. His dark gaze followed her as she approached, and she felt heat rise in her cheeks. It was different out here— on a ranch, away from the city. Everything seemed more basic, more pared down. And when a man's gaze followed her like that, it was harder to ignore.

"Good morning," he said. "Bert's with the babies, so we've got some time."

"Is he getting paid for that?" Ember asked, stepping past Casey's broad chest and into the warm, fragrant barn. Dust motes danced in the air in front of her, and her nose tickled. High windows let in squares of morning sunlight, and it took a moment for her eyes to adjust.

"Of course," Casey said, slamming the door shut. "He's getting overtime. Most expensive childcare ever. I asked if his wife might be interested, but she's got her hands full with her elderly mother, so…"

Casey led the way down the center of the barn. Most of the stalls were empty. He paused at one stall and held a hand out toward a horse's velvet nose. The horse nudged his hand and nickered.

"How much riding experience do you have?" Casey asked, glancing back at her. Again, that dark look trained on her face in that way that made her feel slightly self-conscious.

"None," she admitted.

"Okay, so not Captain, then," he said, moving on. "Captain is fast and strong, but he needs an experienced rider."

"That's not me," she agreed. "Can't we drive?"

"Drive?" Casey turned toward her again, his eyebrows raised. "Not where I'm headed. Why—you scared of horses or something?"

"No, I just thought—" She didn't know what she was thinking. She'd rather feel more in control.

"You don't have to come along, you know," Casey said. "I'm going to check a gate latch out toward Milk River. You said you were interested in that area—"

"No, I want to come along," she interrupted. "I'm fine. Let's do this."

"I'll let you ride Patience here. She's gentle."

That sounded a little better, and Ember watched as Casey led a brown mare from her stall and stroked her glossy neck.

"Good morning, girl," Casey murmured. "You up for a ride today?"

Ember leaned against a rail as she watched Casey saddle the horse. He worked quickly, all the while talking softly to the animal.

"Mr. Vern mentioned that five of the horses would be suited for trail rides with clients," Ember said.

"Patience isn't included in the sale. She's mine," Casey said when he'd finished. "I bought her myself about ten years ago."

"Oh." Ember nodded quickly. "Of course. Sorry, I didn't mean to be presumptuous."

"Never mind. Come around front. You can pet her and introduce yourself."

Ember circled around to the front of the horse and looked up into those gentle, liquid eyes.

"Hello," Ember said softly.

"Now, let me help you mount," Casey said. "Here. Foot in this stirrup. Can you reach? Hold on." He grabbed a wooden box and put it down next to the horse. "Stand on this. Now, foot in the stirrup."

Ember did as he instructed.

"Hand on the pommel— There," Casey coached. "Now, up and swing that leg over."

It wasn't exactly graceful, but a moment later, Ember was settled in the saddle, and Casey gave her a quick look over.

"Good. We're ready," he said, walking over to the far, rolling door. He pushed it open and whistled sharply. A tall, proud horse trotted up, already saddled, and Casey caught the reins. He took a rifle from a corner and slung the strap for it over his back, then put his boot in the stirrup.

Ember gave her horse a little kick in the sides, and nothing happened, save a slightly annoyed shuffle from the horse. Was she supposed to kick harder?

Casey swung up into his saddle effortlessly, and he turned to shoot her a smile. "You ready?"

"How do I get the horse to start moving?" she asked, heat rising in her cheeks. At least she'd warned him that she had no experience.

"Oh, you don't," Casey said with a low laugh. "Patience is my horse, and she'll do what I tell her. You just hold on."

So Ember was literally just along for the ride here… Great.

Casey made a clucking sound with his mouth, and Patience plodded forward toward him. The sensation was a strange one—feeling the movement of the muscles of this empathetic animal, and Ember sucked in a breath.

"I told you that I'd be giving you an honest tour of this ranch," Casey said over his shoulder. "And I'm making good on that."

She's most definitely a city slicker, Casey thought as he stole one last look over his shoulder. A dose of reality might go a long way into showing her exactly what she was getting into here. This was a functioning ranch—a thing of beauty, in Casey's humble opinion. But also rugged, wild and not so easily tamed for her purposes. Shutting down the cattle operation wouldn't change that.

Wolves and coyotes didn't respect lines on a map. Those boundaries had to be patrolled by men who know how to shoot. There were a hundred things she hadn't even thought of yet, he was sure.

And yet, while she might be clueless, that woman was beautiful, too. He could tell that he was softening toward her. There was something about the way her emotions played out in her sparkling blue eyes… He tried to push the thought back. If he met her in any other situation, he'd want to talk to her, get to know her better…figure out if there was a boyfriend in the mix.

Casey leaned down and pulled on the latch to the gate, swinging it open. Ember rode through first—or maybe he should say Patience did, carrying Ember with her—and then Casey rode out, slamming the gate shut behind him. The latch dropped back into place with a satisfying rattle.

"I'm going to take you through the trails," Casey said. "On the other side is pasture, and that's the fence I need to take a look at."

"Where's the river?" she asked.

"You'll see it from the fence." Far down below—but it would give her an idea, at least. "This way." He clucked his tongue, and Patience picked up her pace, catching up with him.

They rode along the gravel road for several minutes, a chilled breeze slipping comfortably past. Casey had always enjoyed this ride—he came out and fixed damaged parts of the fence each spring. But this year was different than the others. Wyatt and Will had brought a certain grounding to his life that he hadn't had before. Everything seemed to matter more in the light of his responsibility toward them.

"You're doing okay," Casey said, glancing over at Ember next to him. She was still sitting rather tensely in the saddle, and she looked over at him.

"Relax," he said. "Let your joints move. You're not going to fall off. You're fine."

"Easier said than done," she observed with a breathy laugh, but he could see her attempt at relaxing her position. "Oh, that is better."

"You've got to trust the horse," he said. "She's not going to listen to you anyway."

Ember smiled ruefully. "You should know that I don't go with the flow very well."

"Yeah, I guessed that," he replied.

"I like things planned. I like to know what's coming."

"Then a ranch isn't good for you," he cautioned.

"Trying to talk me out of this again?" she retorted.

"Maybe," he agreed. "But mostly, I'm just pointing out the obvious. You say you want to take advantage of the great outdoors, but you can't plan so much when it comes to land and weather. Storms come, seasons change. You can't sweat it. You just…wait."

"But you're still prepared," she countered.

"I'll give you that," he agreed, then nodded ahead. "Up there—that's where we enter the trails."

It was nothing more than an opening in a tree line, and Casey pulled the reins, guiding his mount toward it.

"That's it?" Ember sounded less sure of herself now, and when Casey looked over at her, he caught the uncertainty in those blue eyes, too. "How wide are these trails?"

"Wide?" Casey laughed. "Wide enough for a horse, but watch the branches. They can slap you in the face if you don't pay attention."

This would be a lot easier if Miss Ember Reed was a little less attractive. There was something about her that made him want to act the protector. The male side of him wanted to guide her through all of this and make it easy for her. Except she wasn't just a woman out of her depth, and she certainly wasn't a romantic option—she was his direct competition. So he'd better tamp down those chivalrous instincts if he knew what was good for him.

Casey plunged into the foliage first, and he glanced back to see Patience and Ember coming up behind. He ducked his head under a twig and dug his heels into his horse's sides. The woods were cooler than out in the direct sunlight, and the twitter of birds silenced for a moment, and then started up again in a hesitant chatter.

"It's beautiful, isn't it?" he said.

"Yeah…"

He looked back again and saw her gaze moving around them. "How safe is it in here?"

"Safe?" Casey chuckled. "Why do you think I brought a gun?"

"Har har." She shot him a mildly amused look. "You said you'd deal straight with me, and I'm asking as a potential buyer here. How safe are these woods?"

"I wasn't joking," he replied. "This is a hungry time of year for everything—including wolves. Nothing is risk-free out here. But I'm sure you'd have your clients sign a form that saves you from lawsuits."

Ember fell silent, and Casey allowed his horse to pick his path over roots as they made their way through the familiar maze of trails. They weren't all visible anymore—some hadn't been used in years. But a trained eye like Casey's could spot them still. He felt a twinge of guilt. He'd decided to give her an honest tour of this ranch, but it wasn't fair to scare her unduly, either. He wasn't that kind of man.

"You're safe with me, though," he added grudgingly. "I'm a good shot."

"That's why I want to hire you if I do buy this land," she said.

Hire him… Yeah, that wouldn't work well. Not if she'd bought this land out from under his boots and turned it into some city folk feelings center. Not a chance.

He didn't answer her—he'd turned her down once already, and he wasn't about to turn the next week or two into some lengthy argument about his reasoning, either. He'd made his choice, and that was that. But there was something about that woman behind him— city slicker though she was—that made him want to open up more, talk, just to hear her say something in reply. He wouldn't give in to it, though.

They rode in silence for a few more minutes, and then the dense green of trees began to brighten, and in the distance, Casey could make out the glitter of sunlight.

"We're almost out," Casey said, mostly just as an excuse to say something to her.

"Good," she said. "It's a bit eerie in here."

Casey's horse picked up his pace as they got nearer to the tree line, and a moment later, they erupted into sunlight. He reined in his horse, and Ember came out next to him. She looked ready to say something, but then she saw what he'd been waiting to show her.

Grassy hills rolled out beneath them, some rocky piles jutting up from the grass here and there. This used to be plowed land back when people first settled, and those groups of rocks had been made by picking them out of the soil and tossing them, one by one, into those piles. A creek cut between two hills, and to the east there was a marshland with reeds and birds rising up in mesmerizing clouds. The morning sunlight splashed over the scene, and Ember's eyes glistened.

"Oh, my…" she breathed.

"You see that rise over there?" Casey pointed ahead, and Ember followed his finger. "That's where the fence is."

"This is beautiful land," she murmured.

"It's beautiful, but it's rugged," he said. "When we bring the cattle this way to graze, we need cowboys on duty with guns."

Casey clicked his tongue, and they started down the incline at an easy pace.

"Mr. Vern told me last night why he needs to sell this land," Ember said. "He told me about it, but do you know?"

"Of course I do. His wife is suffering from Alzheimer's, and he's used up his insurance. He wants to keep her in a quality care center."

"So even if I don't end up buying this land, someone will," Ember said. "Mr. Vern needs to sell. I'm not the bad guy here, Casey."

Casey eyed her for a moment, wondering how much to say. "I didn't call you bad," he said. "I just said I don't agree with what you stand for."

"Like what, exactly?" she demanded. "Therapy? You might not need someone to talk things out with, but some people do. There's no shame in having some professional help in sorting out difficulties."

"There are plenty of places to get therapy. This is ranching land," he said.

"And it could be set to other uses, too," she said. "And it very well might, depending on who buys it."

She was making a good point. Except she hadn't hit on the reason why he was taking this so personally. It wasn't only about therapy and changing good ranch land into something so unsuited to this place. This wasn't just about a stubborn man and his ideals. This was personal.

"If you don't buy this ranch, I will," he said, his voice low.

Ember blinked at him in surprise. "What?"

"You heard me," Casey said. "I can't afford to pay what you can—and that's why you've got Mr. Vern's priority. The money matters. He needs to get as much as he can for this land. But if you decide against this ranch, I've got an offer on the table behind yours."

"You want to buy it—" she said weakly.

"Yeah." And *want* was a wimpy word. He longed to buy this land on a bone-deep level. He loved every square acre of this place, and if he was going to be raising kids, he couldn't think of a finer place to do it.

"If this is the site of my family's homestead, though—" she began.

"Then you'll buy it," he confirmed. "And I'll understand your attachment to the dirt under your feet. It'll be a connection to generations past—I'm not unfeeling here. But if you don't buy this ranch, then I will, and I'll raise those boys here, teach them about hard work and perseverance. I could have a story here, too—moving into the future."

Casey urged his horse a little faster, pulling out ahead of her. He didn't want her to see the emotion in his eyes. This mattered to him just as much as it mattered to her, and he wasn't going to just walk away from a chance at owning this land himself.

"So I *am* the bad guy," she called from behind him. "To you, at least."

Casey turned in his saddle and met her gaze. "From my perspective, you're just another Reed. You're playing in a different league. You've got money behind you that I couldn't even hope for. And unless you change your mind about this place, there's no doubt that you'll have your way. Reeds always do."

She dealt in feelings and relationships—let her sort that one out.

But Casey was also a Christian, and he stood by his word. They had an agreement, and they'd shaken on it.

She'd help him, and he'd give her an honest introduction to Vern Acres.

Fair was fair.

Chapter Four

Ember sucked in a wavering breath as Casey urged his horse forward again. Her heart hammered in her chest as this new information rattled around inside her. Casey wanted this land, too… It sure explained his chilliness toward her, but it complicated their professional balance, as well. He was just supposed to be a tour guide, not someone with a personal investment in stopping her plan.

Her horse started forward, too, picking up her pace as she plodded along behind Casey's down the rocky slope. He wanted a future here, and she craved a connection to the past—but their dreams were mutually exclusive. The only thing tipping the scales in her favor was that she had more money to give to make her dream come true. She could sympathize with a man who didn't come with the same financial backing she did, because she hadn't always had these opportunities, either, and she had no idea how long they'd last.

Ember's relationship to her father was a fragile one—even if it satisfied a part of her that had always longed to know her dad. Alistair Reed had expectations of his own, and a family pride that she threatened to tarnish by her very existence. Her father's wife, Birdie, had been furious when she found out about Ember. Birdie saw Ember as a threat to her marriage, even though Ember hadn't been the menace—her mother had been, and that affair had ended years ago. But Birdie would take any excuse to drive Ember away and sever the financial cord. Ember wondered what role her stepmother had played in the pressure for Ember to give up her child. Had Birdie been banking on Ember choosing her baby?

That thought clamped down on her heart. *I should have chosen my son. I should have told my father that I was keeping him, and that I'd find a way...*

Again—at the least opportune time—she was thinking about her child. But this wasn't the time or the place to delve into all of that. When she'd made a decision about this land and gone back home, then she could use her last week of leave from work to do some real soul-searching. She could promise herself that much. But not in front of Casey Courtright—the man who wanted to buy this ranch, too.

Patience caught up to Casey once more and Ember felt the heat rise in her cheeks when he looked over at her.

"I couldn't hang back if I wanted to," she said.

He smiled faintly, then shrugged. "We had to face that eventually. Better to lay it out straight."

The horses fell into pace together, and Ember let her gaze move over the countryside. Copses of trees and rock piles broke up the pasture. She breathed out a sigh, wondering if there was a more beautiful place anywhere on God's green earth. If this was the land her family had settled, then she understood why they'd been willing to battle the elements, the wild animals and even unsavory neighbors just to make this land their home.

The thought of neighbors reminded Ember of another problem she faced—the prejudice people around here had against her family name. Would she face pushback from the community? It was possible, but it didn't seem entirely fair. Maybe Reed Land Holdings didn't have many fans out here, but her father was more than just a company. He was a human being.

"Did you ever meet my father?" Ember asked.

"Nope, never did. He sent lawyers to do his dirty work," Casey replied.

Of course. That actually stood to reason. And perhaps it made him easier to hate, too. She'd had her own prejudices against him when she'd first learned that he was her father.

"He's not a bad man," Ember said. "He supports a lot of state charities. Everyone seems to like him."

"Everyone?" Casey raised an eyebrow.

"Except people out here, maybe," she conceded. "But I do understand. When my mother told me who my father was, I wasn't thrilled, either. He has the image of being very aloof and cold, but he's not like that deep down."

"When did your mother tell you about him?" he asked.

"I was seventeen, and she had stage four lung cancer," Ember replied softly. "She wanted me to know who my father was before she left me alone in the world. I knew my father's last name was Reed, since my mother had given me his name, but she'd never told me who he was. She'd been the housekeeper on the Reed estate back then, and when she got pregnant with me, she quit and went away. My father had a family, after all. Anyway, it turned out that he'd known about me all those years, but he'd never reached out to meet me."

"I'm sure he provided financially," Casey countered.

"Not much," she replied. "He helped Mom out a bit, but not enough that I ever saw any. It got sucked up in rent and food and the like. We pinched pennies."

"And you're standing by him being such a good guy," Casey said dryly.

"People change, Casey. And my dad softened up when his youngest son died in Afghanistan. He didn't want to waste any more time when it came to his kids, including me. He rearranged his priorities."

"And the rest of his family?" Casey eyed her from beneath the brim of his hat.

"Were less excited," she said with a dry laugh. "His wife can't stand me. His other kids see me as a drain on their inheritance. My father paid for my education and then gave me this piece of swamp in Florida. None of his other kids wanted it, but then I managed to sell it for a decent amount of money—and that's what I've got behind me right now. So I doubt I'll have anything else coming my way from my father, if his wife and kids can help it. I have enough to buy this land and start up my therapy center. But after that, I'd better start making a profit, because I'm not swimming in endless privilege like you assume. Still, I didn't want to meet my father for his money. It was never about that for me."

Casey was silent, and she couldn't help but wonder how much he was judging her now.

"Are you close to him?" Casey asked as they dropped down into a small valley, and then climbed back upward toward the ridge and faint line of fencing.

"Uh—" That was a loaded question. "I'm glad to finally know my father."

"That doesn't answer me," he replied.

"He's doing his best to make up for not being in my life in my childhood."

"Not by giving you equal consideration with his other children," Casey countered.

"No, that's true, but what I really want from my father isn't financial. I want—" Her voice trembled, and she paused, swallowed. This was getting too personal too quickly. "It doesn't matter what I want. He's not the monster that you seem to think. He's a man who made a big mistake by cheating on his wife, and he's had to make that up to his family, too. He works hard, he's very smart and he has a really strong sense of family pride."

"So strong that he gave you a piece of swampland in Florida that no one wanted," Casey countered. "But if you want a connection to him so badly, why sell the land he gave you? Why come here?" Casey asked.

"Because my mother was the only family I had for seventeen years, and my pride for her isn't dimmed because of my father's money or her past mistake," she shot back. "I have family pride, too, and the stories I heard growing up were all from the Harper side. I might have a wealthy father, but I'm my mother's daughter."

Casey nodded slowly. "Good answer, Miss Reed."

Had she just earned a little bit of his respect, there? "My point is, my father has his own challenges to deal with, and I'm not some prissy heiress. We're all just people, doing our best. Including my dad."

"Hmm." Casey cast her an indecipherable look. "I like you better as the proud daughter of a housekeeper."

"Well, I'm more complicated than that," she retorted. Chances were, he was more complicated than he was letting on, too, but she wasn't expecting him to open up.

Casey chuckled softly. "All right, all right."

"Everyone makes mistakes, Casey."

Everyone, including her. And mistakes couldn't be undone. That was the problem with too many of them—they were so final. Would her son resent her decision, too? Would she ever be able to admit why she gave him up? At the age of twenty, everything seemed a whole lot more dire than it did now. But then, she now had an education, a career, a home… Things *were* more dire back then.

They came up the last of the incline, a few pebbles clattering down the hill behind them, and Casey reined his horse in. He dismounted, in one smooth motion, then came around his horse toward her.

"You aren't what I expected," he said quietly.

She smiled slightly and sighed. No one ever was. She'd learned that when she counseled families. Under all the mistakes and external shells lay soft, vulnerable human beings.

"You want to dismount, or stay where you are?" he asked after a moment of silence.

Her muscles were already strained and sore from the position they'd been holding the last little while. Getting down and walking around for a bit sounded good, but she looked at the ground uncertainly. It was a long drop, and there was no handy wooden box out here.

"I don't know…" she said.

"Come on." He held a hand aloft. "I'll help you down."

"But how will I get back up again?" she asked with a breathy laugh.

"I'll get you up there." He eyed her, squinting slightly in the sunlight, and her heart sped up just a little bit. She looked around them, her gaze moving over the rolling hills, the rocky stretches...feeling just how alone they were out here.

"How do I do this?" she asked at last.

"Take your other foot out of the stirrup, and stand up on this leg." She felt his hand tap her ankle. "Patience can take it. She's fine. So all your weight—this leg."

Ember did as he said and swung her leg back over the saddle. It was a long way down, and as she started her descent, her stomach leaped to her throat. She landed in a strong pair of arms before her boot hit the ground, and the air squeezed out of her lungs.

Casey was stronger than she'd thought, because he supported the full weight of her while she got her feet back underneath her, and boosted her back into balance. For a moment, she felt his strong chest against her back, and the steady pounding of his heart thudded slow and steady. Then she was upright again, and he stepped away.

"That wasn't graceful," she breathed.

"Not at all," he said with a short laugh, and when she turned, he raised his hands. "Hey, who says you have to be graceful all the time, huh?"

Casey went to his saddlebag and pulled out a hammer, a plastic bag of what appeared to be nails and a pair of work gloves.

"Look, I don't mean to insult your father," Casey

said and cleared his throat. "There have been some pretty serious consequences to his success around here, so I'm not going to pretend I like what he's done, but I can understand that he's your dad, and you're going to have a different experience of him."

"Thank you."

"Still, you've got to understand that while your father got richer, a lot of us lost our family's legacies. So." He shrugged, then turned away. "I'm going to fix the latch on the gate."

Casey headed past the horses and down another incline toward the fence. Most of it was barbed wire, but in the center was a tall wooden gate that swung loose in the wind, the hinges creaking. Ember watched as he worked on the broken latch for a few minutes. He was silent, but in the wide outdoors, constant speaking didn't seem necessary. It was companionable, and she realized that she liked Casey's company. Casey finished with the gate, then tested it a couple of times before ambling back to his horse to replace the tools in his saddlebag.

"Where's Milk River?" she asked.

"Come here." Casey went to the fence again and waited while she made her way down the rocky terrain. He pulled off his work gloves, then nudged his hat up higher on his forehead as she reached his side. He smelled musky and warm, and even a few inches away from him she was aware of just how tall he was. "See down there—" He leaned a little closer so that she could follow his pointing arm. "Past the trees, there's a glittery patch—"

Ember looked the direction he pointed, and she spotted the glitter he was referring to.

"I see it."

"That's water. The trees grow by the bank, and it's dug its way down pretty deep over the years, so the banks are steep and high over there. But that's Milk River."

Somehow, it seemed less impressive than she'd built it up to be in her head, and she let out a pent-up breath. "Oh."

Casey paused, tensed, his gaze still locked in the same place. He didn't move, and Ember looked up at him hesitantly.

"What's wrong?" she asked.

"I'm staring at a wolf right now." His voice was calm—too calm for her comfort—and he slowly turned, scanning the landscape. "I only see one right now. The others might be hiding, or it could be a lone scout. Either way, we're moving out."

Ember squinted, looking in the direction he was, and then she saw it—a tuft of gray on the other side of that glitter of water. It stood tall and motionless, then turned and paced a couple of times before stopping and staring in their direction once more.

Casey pointed to her horse. "Let's go. Saddle up."

Ember headed for her horse, lifted her leg to get one foot in the stirrup and felt strong hands around her waist propelling her upward. With a gasp of surprise, she fumbled but managed to get her leg up over the saddle and turned to see Casey already moving toward his own horse, looking over his shoulder in the direction of the wolf.

"It's pretty far away," Ember said, trying to keep the tremor out of her voice.

"Let's keep it that way," Casey replied, and he pulled

his gun off his back and reached into his saddlebag, coming out with two shells. "You go first." He slapped Patience's rump. "Go home, Patience."

The horse didn't need to be told twice, and Ember lowered herself over the saddle as they headed up to the tree line once more.

"Lord, protect us," she whispered, but when she glanced back, she saw Casey with a rifle in one hand and his dark gaze scanning the landscape. If anything was going to come at them, she had a feeling she was in good hands.

Casey urged his horse faster as they approached the tree line. He looked back, surveying the countryside from his higher vantage point, but the wolf had disappeared, and he couldn't see any more movement. Still, wolves blended into their environments rather easily, and he wouldn't feel right until he had Ember back on the other side of the woods where wolves didn't dare approach.

It was one thing to be looking out for himself and another ranch hand who knew how to deal with these things, and quite another to have a completely green city girl on his hands. One day he'd get married, but in his mind's eye, his wife would be just as good a shot as he was. This land required respect and a steady trigger finger. That was a lesson he'd be teaching the boys when they got old enough to hold their own guns…

Ember put an arm up, pushing some twigs away from her face as Patience carried her into the forest. He took one last look behind them before he followed her into the woods.

"Are we in any danger?" Ember asked, looking over her shoulder at him.

"I wasn't about to stick around and give the wolves any ideas," Casey replied. "We can shoot them if they harass us or the cattle, but they're endangered, too, so I'm not about to start taking potshots at wolves if I don't have to."

She turned back to face forward, and he was struck by the shine to her blond waves that fell over her shoulder and down her back. A twig was caught in her hair, and Casey had the urge to pluck it out, but he wasn't close enough. She was a beautiful woman, but also vulnerable. A country woman wouldn't be quite so reliant on him for safety and common sense out here, and he felt the weight of that responsibility.

They rode in silence through the woods until they emerged on the other side into the scattered shade at the forest edge.

"The wolves never come this close to a human settlement," Casey said. "Not in daylight."

"Shouldn't you be able to do more about the wolves?" Ember asked.

"Yeah, if you buy this place, the wolves are your problem, too," Casey said with a rueful smile. "But they're an important part of the ecosystem out here.

"Like I said before, it's not about your convenience out here. It's about finding a way to live alongside nature safely."

"I get it."

Did she? He wasn't so certain.

Casey let his eyes roam over the patchwork of fields and those gently snaking roads that made their way between them. He'd driven every single one of those roads, and he knew these fields—the kinds of grass that grew in them, the drainage when the snow melted, the state of the fences that surrounded them—like the back of his hand. If only he'd known his boss as well. He understood that things had deteriorated quickly for Mrs. Vern, but his boss had kept that private for a long time, too. He hadn't opened up, shared a bit, given Casey any indication that he should be scraping some money together to make an offer that could compete with what a Reed brought to the table.

Everyone looked out for themselves, it seemed. Even Christians. Even country folk. Everyone kept their personal business close to the vest and tried to sort out their own situation.

Casey, people might like you a whole lot, but they like their own hide more, his father used to tell him. Funny how it took a couple of decades for wisdom to grow deep.

When they got back to the barn, he dismounted, then helped Ember down from Patience's back. She rubbed her legs and stretched—definitely not used to the exertion of horseback riding, and he turned his attention to unsaddling the horses and turning them out to pasture for the rest of the day.

"Mr. Vern invited us up for lunch at the house," Casey said, then paused. "Hold on—" He reached behind her back and plucked that twig out of her hair. It took a moment to untangle it, and her hair felt silky in his calloused hands. He held the twig up as proof that he'd had an excuse to touch her.

She smiled feebly. "I'm not scared off, Casey."

"I'm not trying to scare you," he replied, feeling

mildly offended that she'd think so. "You saw the wolf, didn't you?"

She eyed him for a moment. "You're a ranch manager here. What would make working for me so different?"

"First of all, you wouldn't be ranching," he retorted.

"Fine. But I have a feeling that even if I were intent on raising cattle, you'd still have a problem with working for me."

Casey headed for the door, pushed it open and waited for Ember to leave the barn ahead of him. "My family had a ranch, and we'd been on that land for three generations. Reed Land Holdings ran us out of business, then bought the ranch when we couldn't hang on any longer."

Ember stepped outside into the spring chill, then turned back to look at him, some combination of uncertainty and compassion swimming in those blue eyes.

"When was this?"

"Fifteen years ago. I got a job here and worked my way up—not because I have a passion for ranching someone else's land, but because I had no other choice. And now I've got the boys to raise, and no land of my own to do it on."

"What happened to your father's ranch had nothing to do with me, you know."

"It's your family," he said.

"But not *me*." She met his gaze almost defiantly.

"It's your family's money," he said. "And forgive me for being picky about that detail, but it amounts to the same thing. I get that you aren't some spoiled rich girl in the deepest sense, but you're a part of the machine, and you're looking to take a running ranch and turn it into something completely different. There will be ripples. This will affect a lot more than you think."

"And a good number of those ripples might be positive," she said with a shake of her head. "Turning this place into a therapy center isn't about me and my career. This is about something I owe to God."

"What's that?" he asked, softening his tone.

"I promised I'd do everything I could to strengthen families. If He helped me to get the education I needed, I'd take every penny that came from my tarnished family and put it back into building other people back up. I'm sorry this isn't about cattle, Casey. Maybe you'd approve if I cared more about cows. But I am going to build something important here. This is about people."

She carried on toward the truck, leaving Casey to catch up this time, and he shook his head. They'd never see eye to eye on this, but she was convinced that she was doing something good and moral. There was no one more stubborn than a do-gooder. He picked up his pace and met her at the vehicle.

"Let's go," he said, hopping into the driver's side. She got in next to him, and as she buckled up her seat belt, he turned the key and snapped his own strap into place.

When they got to the house, Mr. Vern was waiting. He met them with a cordial nod and stepped back as they came into the kitchen.

"So what did you think of what you've seen so far?" Mr. Vern asked as Ember took off her jacket and hung it on a hook. The smell of tomato soup and toasted BLTs met them.

"It's a beautiful area," Ember said. "Breathtaking, really."

"That it is," Mr. Vern agreed. "And that's only a tiny taste."

The old cowboy pulled a pot of soup off the stove. Sandwiches already waited on the table, cut diagonally and stacked on a plate. Mr. Vern ladled soup into a bowl and brought it to the table, then headed back to the stove. He moved slowly, purposefully.

"Have a seat," Mr. Vern said.

It wasn't Casey's place to be served by the boss, but Ember sat down in a chair and looked hungrily at the spread before them.

"Let me finish that up, sir," Casey said.

"Nonsense. Sit down, Casey. How was your ride?"

"It was cut short," Ember said. "There was a wolf eyeing us."

"Linda always hated them," Mr. Vern said, coming back to the table with the last two bowls in his hands. Some soup slopped over the side of one bowl as he placed them on the table, and Casey dropped a napkin over the spill. "Before they passed the law protecting wolves, we had a whole herd of migrating elk that moved through in the fall. We had a decent income from hunters coming to hunt on our land, and we offered a guide service. But not anymore. The herd isn't so big anymore, and they move through fast. The wolves make sure of that."

Ember frowned slightly, looking over at Mr. Vern with questions in her eyes. Casey's mind wasn't on the wolves, though. They were an old problem. He was wondering how the babies were doing. Funny how he'd started to worry about them when he was gone.

"Let's pray," Mr. Vern said, bowing his head. "For this food we are about to eat, make us truly thankful."

He raised his head, nudged the plate of sandwiches toward Ember, then picked up his spoon. The older man's hand trembled, and he put the spoon back down.

"Everything all right, sir?" Casey asked.

"Fine," he growled, and Casey eyed him a moment longer. That was a lie, but maybe he didn't want to talk in front of Ember. Casey nodded, then took a mouthful of soup, watching his boss from the corner of his eye. After a beat or two, Mr. Vern sighed.

"I got a call from the care home," he said, his voice tight. "Linda had a bad morning. They couldn't calm her down. They needed my permission to sedate her."

"What was she upset about?" Ember asked.

"Don't know," Mr. Vern replied. "Something about getting dressed. She didn't want to be touched." He sucked in a wavering breath. "I'd have her here with me, but she kept wandering off, and the last time I found her, she was by herself in three feet of snow wearing nothing but her pajamas and holding a cookie sheet."

Silence descended around the table.

"When we were kids, we used to sled on cookie sheets," Mr. Vern said, then cleared his throat. "Maybe she saw the snow and in her mind… Anyway."

Mr. Vern picked up his spoon again and took a mouthful of soup. Casey and Ember followed his lead, but Casey's stomach no longer wanted the sustenance. He could see the pain in the older man's eyes. And he knew that it was more than just his wife's problems that morning. The bills were climbing, and as his boss had told him earlier, he was in debt.

"I'm a licensed therapist," Ember said after a moment. "If you wanted to talk about it—"

"No," Mr. Vern said with a bitter laugh. "I appreciate the offer, young lady, but I don't need to be asked how I feel. I know how I feel, and I don't want to talk about it. I'll go visit my wife. She'll be sedated, but I think there will be a part of her that will know I'm there."

Ember fell into silence, and Casey met her gaze for a moment. She needed to understand that people out here were different. Tougher, maybe, and more self-sufficient. She was right that everyone had their personal issues, but not everyone wanted to talk about it. Sometimes, a man just needed enough dirt under his boots to soak up the pain.

"I'm sorry—" Mr. Vern stood up. "I hope you'll understand if I head down to the city now. It's a long drive, and I need to see Linda for myself—know that she's okay. You stay and eat. Just lock up on your way out, if you don't mind, Casey."

Casey pushed back his chair. "Absolutely, sir. Do what you need to do."

That kind of love was a precious thing, and while the price was this kind of heartbreak at the end of that love story, it made a life deeper and more meaningful for the years of devotion.

Casey had two little babies waiting for him back at his house, boys he'd determined to raise, and he wondered if they'd creep into his heart like that... become his meaning for all the hard work. Because that was what a family was, wasn't it? And he was doing his best—taking care of the babies, trying to arrange things so that he could give them the best childhood possible. He'd be their dad—or at the very least he'd be the only dad they'd remember. Still, he couldn't help but wonder how long it would take before they truly felt like his.

Chapter Five

They finished eating after Mr. Vern left, then wrapped up the leftover food and put it in the fridge. Mr. Vern would be hungry eventually, and Ember wondered if there was any way she could help this man in his time of need. Except he didn't want her help—that seemed to be a theme out here. Even Casey didn't seem to want her well-intentioned offering of a job. Would it be so miserable to work with her for a little while until he sorted out something better? She didn't want to turn his life upside down. She was trying to be reasonable here.

Before they left to go back to Casey's house, Ember made some phone calls to two different local historical societies. She'd asked them to look into the records to see who owned this plot of land going back as far as possible. So far, they had owners going back seventy-five years, but back in 1981, there was a big flood that had damaged a lot of the antique records. She'd hoped that coming out here might give her access to records that weren't readily available online, but that didn't look likely right now.

"Any news?" Casey asked her when she hung up after her last call.

"No," she admitted with a sigh. "But I'm not giving up quite yet."

"Didn't think you would." He smiled ruefully. "Let's get back to the house."

Once at the ranch manager's house, Bert left for his own shift at work, leaving Ember and Casey alone with the infants. Ember ruminated over her challenge to find some evidence about who settled this land while she focused on the tasks at hand: diapers, bottles, sleeping. Casey put in a load of laundry, and Ember set to washing a sink load of baby bottles. She'd known it wouldn't be easy to track her family's holdings, but it seemed like every time she had an idea, she hit another roadblock.

And while she agonized over her own problems, that old rancher was off visiting his ailing wife. She felt a pang at her own selfishness. Was that the Reed in her?

"I feel for Mr. Vern," Ember said, raising her voice a little so that Casey could hear her in the other room.

"Me, too," Casey said, and he ambled over to the doorway of the kitchen. "This is a tough time for him."

"How long have he and his wife been married?" she asked.

"I don't know. Since they were about 18, I think. He told me once that he met her in high school."

"That's sweet… I come across couples who have been together since high school in my practice. It used to be a regular occurrence. Not anymore."

"You mean marriages lasting that long?" Casey asked.

"Marriages that started that young that last so long,"

she amended. "But when it lasts, there is a really beautiful bond that only comes with time together."

"But the ones you're seeing are coming for therapy," Casey pointed out.

"I never said it had to be marriage counseling," she said, shooting him a rueful smile over her shoulder. "The last couple I met with who had been together that long were working through grief over the loss of—" She swallowed, biting off the words.

"Loss of what?" Casey prodded.

"Family land," she finished, and a wash of guilt came over her. Land could mean something to various different people, but only one person could actually own it. It didn't matter who won this—someone else would lose.

Even in adoption, in order for Pastor Mitchell and his wife to adopt her son, she'd had to give him up. And they'd been trying for a decade to get pregnant, they told her. Nothing had worked. The wife—Sue—had told Ember a little bit about her struggle. She said that all she'd ever wanted was a big family...

Ember's mind continued to wander as she plunged her rubber-gloved hands into the hot, sudsy water. In order for Ember to gain some feeling of connection to her biological father, she'd had to tear into a perfectly happy family. Birdie hated Ember because she'd only found out about her husband's affair when Ember showed up after her mother's death. Then Alistair had been forced to confess it all to his wife and kids. So in order for Ember to have a relationship with her dad, her half siblings had to learn the ugly truth that their father had cheated on their mother. In order for anyone to take a step forward, it felt like there was a cost to be paid by someone else. Hardly fair, but the way the world worked—only one person could "win" at a time.

Back then, when her mother died, Ember hadn't been thinking clearly enough to consider consequences—the consequences of meeting her father...and of other things. She'd hated facing life on her own, and she'd had one surefire way to numb everything—parties.

So that fateful night during her second year of college, Ember sneaked out to a party, as she'd done so many times in the past. The next morning, she'd woken up in a confused fog on a strange couch, and missing some rather important articles of clothing. Had she done what she feared she'd done?

And she'd felt a flood of shame. Was this what she wanted for the rest of her life? A blur of alcohol and parties...flunking out of college, because she was too hungover to pay attention in class? Was this all she had to look forward to?

Ember had pulled together what she could find of her belongings and headed back to her dorm room. Sitting on the edge of her bed, her head spinning and her stomach churning from the drinking she'd done the night before, she realized that she wanted more...she wanted to be better. Not to impress her father, or punish him—but for herself! She wanted to turn her life around and belong to the one Father she could count on to never stop loving her. And she longed for forgiveness for whatever it was she'd done the night before that left her feeling so soiled and empty. Sitting on the edge of that dorm bed, she'd bowed her head and given her life—as muddled as it was—over to Jesus.

"...if You still want it," she'd whispered.

Unknown to her in that moment, she was already

pregnant. Her change of heart—her desire to be something better—had all come one night too late.

Behind her, one of the babies woke from his sleep, a hiccuping wail piercing the quiet. Ember pulled herself out of her memories and looked over her shoulder. Casey stood by the couch, a laundry basket filled with onesies, sleepers and tiny socks, and he dropped a onesie on top of a pile of folded laundry then headed for the cradle. Just then, the other baby let out a whimper.

"You want to give me a hand?" Casey asked, and Ember dried off.

"Sure." She went to the other cradle and looked down into the scrunched little face. Will waved one tiny fist in the air, his lips quivering and tears welling in his eyes. She bent down and scooped him up, propping him up onto her shoulder. At a few weeks old, he was already bigger than her son had been the last time she'd seen him.

But Will didn't settle. He sucked in great, heaving breaths and wailed with all his might. She tried changing his position, patting his back, rocking…and nothing seemed to work. Both babies cried their hearts out and Ember met Casey's gaze with a panicked look of her own.

"What's the matter with them?" she asked helplessly.

"This happens sometimes," Casey said, raising his voice above the babies' cries.

"What do you do?" she asked, looking down into that red, tear-streaked face of the tiny boy in her arms. She rocked back and forth, swinging her weight from one foot to the other in an instinctive sway. The cries paused for a moment, then started up again, as if the rocking had only been a mild surprise.

"Maybe they miss their mother," Casey said, and Ember froze.

She swallowed, then adjusted Will up onto her shoulder once more so she had an excuse to turn away. Tears pricked her eyes, and she tried to swallow the lump that rose in her throat when she remembered that heart-wrenching cry that had erupted from her own son as his adoptive mother walked away with him.

It's for the best, everyone said. She'd bestowed the gift of life by giving birth to him, and by placing him for adoption she was giving him a family that could provide him more than she could. But what if her baby boy had sobbed his little heart out while strangers tried to comfort him? What if that guttural, heartbroken wail had been her son's only way to call for his mother?

And she'd never come.

This was why she shouldn't be caring for infants—these memories that kept sweeping up and threatening to knock her down. She sucked in a wavering breath as she realized that Will was starting to settle. The baby's cries were softer now, and as she swayed back and forth, his eyes were drifting shut. But Wyatt still wailed from Casey's arms.

"Whatever you're doing, it's working," Casey said with a grin. Then he hesitated. "You okay?"

"Yep." She nodded quickly, keeping up that swaying as her throat thickened with repressed emotion.

"I have a theory," Casey said. Then he nodded to a La-Z-Boy chair in the corner. "Go sit down there—it rocks."

Ember sank into the chair. Will's howls had fully

subsided now, and he buried his wet little face into her neck. He sucked in deep, trembling sighs. If this child was crying in hopes of calling his mama, how long would it be before he forgot her? How long before his tiny heart stopped yearning for the mother who would never come?

Casey eased the wailing Wyatt into her arms on the other side of her chest, and Wyatt sobbed out his grief. Will started to whimper again, and then Casey put a big hand on the back of the chair and started to rock it for her.

"Talk to them," he ordered.

"Uh—" Ember looked down at the frustrated babies and swallowed against the tightness in her throat. "Boys, I want you to stop now. Okay? I want you to be good boys and be quiet for me."

Wyatt blinked up at her in mild confusion, but the crying stopped.

"All right, then," she said quietly. "That's good. Let's not cry just now, okay? Because we're okay. We're going to get through this. It's a feeling, and while feelings are very, very strong, they pass. They aren't forever."

Her words were meant as a reminder for herself—this overwhelming grief she'd been battling, the guilt at the thought that she'd made the wrong choice, or made her choice for the wrong reasons... It wasn't forever. She could wade through it, and she would feel happiness and contentment again. Eventually.

Feelings were not permanent. Feelings did not define her. She might feel like a failure at times, or like she was unworthy after what she'd done, but that was not a fact. The fact was that she had a God who loved her despite her mistakes, and her identity was in Him.

The babies settled into quiet, softly hiccuping as their breathing slowed. Casey kept the chair rocking with his strong arm, and she was struck again by the size of him. Standing over her like that, she could feel his strength and his gentleness contained in that muscular physique—the last thing she wanted to be reminded of just now.

Her emotions were in enough of a muddle without adding a handsome cowboy into the mix, but when she glanced up at him, she saw a wistful look on his face.

"A woman's touch," he murmured.

"Maybe they just tired out," she said.

"Nah, they've gone for way longer than that," he replied with a soft laugh, and his brown eyes sparkled, then faded. He straightened, and Ember took over the rocking of the chair for herself.

The babies were quiet now, their eyes closed, wet lashes brushing their pink cheeks.

"Feelings don't last forever," she whispered against their wispy hair. "You just have to wait them out, and they go away eventually."

One day, they wouldn't remember their mother anymore and they wouldn't yearn for her smell or her voice or her touch… One day, even memories would fade, as she knew would have happened with her own little boy. Her son—named by another woman—would have forgotten her entirely.

It was the mother who couldn't forget.

Casey looked down at the woman in his armchair. Ember leaned her head back, her golden hair tumbling around her shoulders. The babies' eyes had shut, and they slept facing each other as Ember rocked them. She had a hand on each little rump, but her attention seemed like it had wandered away as she looked toward the window and the afternoon sunlight outside. Whenever she held a baby, she seemed to do that—slip mentally away.

It shouldn't matter. The babies were soothed, and it looked like those boys needed the feminine touch—the one thing he couldn't provide. But he'd have to—sooner rather than later. He needed a woman in this with him—a wife to stand by him and help him raise these kids. Maybe a mom in the mix would make this feel more like a proper family.

"Thanks for this," he said, and he sank into the couch opposite her. The room was cozily warm, and he exhaled a tired sigh.

Ember looked over at him and smiled weakly. "No problem."

They were quiet for a couple of beats, and then Ember asked, "How long have you known Mr. Vern? You two seem pretty close."

"Most of my life," Casey said. "He and my dad were friends, and when we lost the ranch, Mr. Vern offered me a job. I've been working here ever since."

"That's why he trusts you so much."

"I'm good at my job because I was raised on a ranch and I was bidding on cattle at the auction by the time I was twelve. My dad showed me the ropes—I know how to run a ranch. So, yeah, he trusts me."

She eyed him for a moment. "But you're not happy here."

Happy wasn't something he'd been worrying about

lately. He'd had a job to do, and land to buy. His happiness was going to come later—at least that was what he told himself.

"It's been a place holder," Casey admitted. "I want to own a ranch, not just run one for someone else. There's something about having your stake in a place—makes a difference. And it isn't that I'm not happy here, because I do love this land. I'm just not happy being only a manager."

She nodded. "I get that."

"You're perceptive," he said, then added with a teasing smile, "for a city girl."

"You aren't so mysterious as you think," she replied with a smile. "It was how you acted in the house—kind of tense and coiled. You're different on horseback."

"Isn't everybody?" he quipped. "But I'm not the only one who isn't happy until I'm my own boss. You're the same way, from what I can see."

She angled her head to the side in acceptance of that. "Actually, I'm just trying to make the most of this before my father cuts me loose."

"You've mentioned that before. Do you think he will?" Casey asked with a frown.

"I know he will," she replied. "His other kids can count on his continued support and an inheritance eventually. He gave me an education and a little money. I'm grateful for it—it's my step up—and I'm not going to squander it. Because after this, I'm sure there won't be any more."

"You're smart," Casey said with a slow nod.

"I am." She smiled ruefully. "But this isn't about money. I'd trade it all in for an actual relationship with my father."

"You aren't what I expected," he admitted.

"Under it all, everyone is surprisingly human," she replied. "That is the one thing I've learned in my years as a therapist."

"So if you aren't terribly close to your family, who are you close to?" Casey asked.

"The money complicated things," she said. "My old friends from high school fell away when I went to college. That happens, of course. And then the friends I made in college got a little jealous when I had privileged problems, like how to make sure I could make enough money off a property sale in order to invest in a new business venture. That sort of thing."

"Their hearts bled for you," he said with a low laugh.

"Something like that." Will moaned in his sleep and Ember patted his back absently. "I'm in a bit of a no-man's-land right now. Even you can't quite decide what you think of me."

Casey had to admit that was true. She was beautiful, insightful, but still stubborn when it came to her own point of view. She'd been on his mind lately, both as his competition, but also as... Dare he think of her as a woman? She was surprisingly human, but it didn't change that she was going to alter the landscape of this ranching country—or that she'd be doing it on the land where he'd hoped to settle down and raise a family.

"Well, in the moment, you're helping me out of a tough spot, so I'm inclined to like you." He shot her a teasing smile. "You want some coffee?"

"Sure."

He pushed himself to his feet and headed into the kitchen. He pulled the plug on the sink full of soapy water on his way past, glancing at the row of freshly washed baby bottles. He'd wanted a woman's touch around here, but he had to admit that it stung when the babies seemed to prefer Ember to him when they wanted comforting.

But whatever. It was help, and he couldn't be picky.

Casey grabbed a coffee filter and the tin of coffee grounds from a cupboard and set to work measuring and filling the coffee maker with water. His hands did the work without any thought, and his mind spun ahead.

"Mind if I ask you a question…professionally?" he asked.

"You mean as a therapist?" she said.

He winced, then turned around. "Yes."

"Shoot."

"When do I tell the boys about their parents? I mean, their death was pretty grisly, and I'd hate to scare little boys. The thought— I don't know. How do I do that?"

"Never hide what happened," she replied. "But there's no need to go into detail. You can tell them a little more as they get older. But I'd recommend starting out with a picture of their parents in the home. Point to it, and tell them that is their first mommy and daddy. If they know from the start that they're adopted and why, there are no big, shocking conversations to have later on."

"Makes sense. I guess I'm a little afraid of being told I'm not their real dad when I tell them to do something."

"Oh, kids come up with all sorts of stuff, even if you are the biological parent," she replied. "Don't be afraid of something they might say later. Besides, if you are always very open about their parents, they won't feel like they're betraying you later when they want to learn more about them."

"Yeah…" He nodded, then sauntered back into the living room. Ember looked down at the sleeping babies, then up at him.

"Help me get them into their cribs?" she said.

"Sure." Casey bent and picked up Will first, freeing up Ember so she could get to her feet. He laid the baby in his cradle and looked down at the little guy. "I guess I'm afraid that they'd be right."

"About what?" she asked, laying Wyatt in the other cradle next to his brother.

"That I'm not their real dad." He looked up at Ember uneasily.

"Because they don't feel like yours yet," she supplied.

He was silent—was that a terrible thing to admit to?

"Casey, I'm going to tell you something," she said, stepping closer and putting a hand on his arm. "I've heard biological parents say the same thing. Childbirth is traumatic. They expect to feel this rush of unblemished love when they look at their baby, but that child is purple, squished and, frankly, a little ugly. They're in shock from the pain, the blood loss, from meeting their child for the first time… And when they get home from the hospital, they are sleep deprived and overwhelmed. They don't feel what they expected to feel. It isn't all picture-perfect and rosy. It's exhausting and scary and a massive change."

"Okay…" he said slowly.

"My point is, you lost your cousin when you became legal guardian of these boys. That's traumatic. You're busy, trying to adjust your life to two infants, and have no idea what your future with them will look like. This wasn't planned. This wasn't anyone's ideal, including yours. And that's okay."

"Is it? I think those boys deserve to be someone's ideal," he said.

"You'll get there."

"I want to."

"You will." She met his gaze evenly, and she seemed convinced of that, at least.

"Yeah." That was all true. Frankly, it was downright scary at the moment. He'd gone from bachelor to single parent of two overnight.

"Stop expecting perfection." She let her hand on his arm drop.

"That's it?" He eyed her.

"That's it." Ember shrugged. "None of us are perfect, Casey. Stop expecting it of yourself. You'll adjust. You'll figure it out. You'll be a good dad."

"What makes you so sure?"

"You cared enough to ask." She shot him a smile, and for the first time she looked relaxed, and that smile lit her features. She went from awfully pretty to stunning, and he swallowed. Ember pulled her hair away from her face with a swipe of her fingers, and he tried not to notice how appealing she was when she relaxed like that.

"Okay," he said feebly.

"That right there—" She waggled a finger at him. "That was therapy."

He rolled his eyes. "Hardly. That was advice."

"Yeah, well, it was advice from a professional, and if you don't get that reassurance, you might worry for nothing, or beat yourself up when you should really be cutting yourself a little slack. Sometimes it helps to have someone else point out that you're doing okay." She eyed him, waiting.

"And this is the gift of therapy that you want to bring the people of this county," he said with a wry smile.

"It isn't such a terrible thing, is it?" She smiled again, her blue gaze meeting his.

"You relax when you're solving other people's problems," he said instead. She did more than relax—she came to life. Not that he'd put it that way out loud.

She blinked, and some of that self-confidence fell away. The smile slipped, the sparkle in her eyes dimmed. He hadn't meant to do that, exactly, and he regretted it. He was just meaning to point out what was obvious to him—she seemed to blossom when sorting out other people's garbage.

"It did…uh…help, though," he offered after a beat of silence.

"You hate that a little bit," she said, a rueful smile curving her lips again.

"Nah…" He chuckled, then shrugged. "I'm a man. I'd rather rub dirt on it and walk it off, but that doesn't always work."

"I daresay it never works," she countered.

"You walk long enough and you forget," he replied with a lift of his shoulders.

"You don't forget, though." The smile evaporated and sadness misted her eyes. She compressed her lips into a line and swallowed. "They tell you that you will—but that's a lie."

Those words were coming from a deeper, more private place inside her, he could tell, and he tried to catch her eye again, but she turned away and headed back into the kitchen, where the coffeepot was burbling away. She grabbed a mug and poured herself a cup prematurely, the drips of coffee hissing on the heater below before she replaced the pot.

"Ember?" he said. "You okay?"

She turned back toward him, recomposed. "I'm fine." She lifted the mug in a salute. "You rub dirt, and I drink coffee."

"You want to talk about it?"

"Not really. It's—" She shook her head. "It's old. I'm fine."

Fair enough. But when he'd seen that pain in her eyes, it made him want to fix it somehow. Maybe that was just the man in him. But he had a feeling that she wouldn't let him, anyway.

Chapter Six

Ember got up early the next morning. Casey had offered to drive her to church with him, and she'd accepted the offer. From what Casey told her, this was the only congregation a comfortable driving distance from the ranch, and most of the Christians in the area attended one of two services in a little country church that wasn't big enough for everyone at one time.

But Ember hadn't agreed to go to church just to see the local parish. She felt like she needed some grounding after her last week. Worship was healing.

Ember heard the rumble of Casey's pickup truck outside the house, and she grabbed her purse, slipped on a pair of strappy heels and went out to meet him. The chill spring air made her shiver as it met her bare legs. She hurried to the passenger side and Casey leaned over and pushed the door open for her.

"Good morning," he said as she hopped up into the cab and the welcome jet of heat.

"Morning." She smiled at him and looked into the back seat. Both babies were sleeping, their soothers rising and falling in a syncopated rhythm. She pulled on her seat belt as Casey started forward again.

They fell into a companionable silence as Casey drove out to the gravel road and turned onto it.

"You seem like an old hand at this," Ember said. "The car seats, the soothers…"

"Oh, that took forty-five minutes," Casey said with a low laugh. "But I had no faith in my ability to do this quickly, so I started early."

Ember chuckled. "You seem to just…roll with these things, though. It's admirable."

"Then I fake it well." He shot her a rueful smile. "I'm pretty overwhelmed here. In fact, I considered not taking the babies to church at all today, but I don't want to start that. I doubt it'll get easier as they get bigger, so it's probably better to just jump in."

Ember smiled. He didn't seem to realize that his attitude was rare. Not a lot of men would just launch themselves into childcare the way he had.

"What about you?" Casey pulled down the visor as he turned onto the highway and the morning sun glistened into their eyes.

"What about me?" she asked, adjusting her visor, too.

"Do you want kids one day?"

Ember sucked in a breath. She was asked this from time to time, and the answer was never easy.

"No," she admitted. "I don't."

"Okay." He nodded, then leaned back in his seat. "I get it. Not everybody wants kids. I always thought I'd be a dad, but after I was married. Not before! This took me by surprise."

"I think babies are wonderful," Ember said. "Don't

get me wrong there! I had a tough time after my mom died, and I had to grow up really fast. When I made that promise to God that if He helped me to get my education, I'd put all of myself into helping others with my career, I took that vow really seriously. I know that I could do that and have a family, but..." How could she explain this without saying too much?

"God doesn't call us all to the same life," Casey concluded.

"Yes, and maybe we aren't all suited to the same things. I do feel called to help others through therapy. I know I can make a difference there."

"I get it."

"Most people tell me I'll change my mind. But you know when you've stepped into stride with God's will. You can feel it."

"It isn't anyone's place to change your mind, Ember," he said. "From what I know of you, you're a woman who's thought things through."

"I have. I've been through a lot, but those experiences help me to understand what others are going through in their rough patches. My clients don't need to feel as alone as I did."

God was the God of second chances. But Ember didn't see motherhood as something in the past—it was very much in the present. She would always be a mother, even if she couldn't raise her son. But having more children felt like a betrayal to the son she gave away. What made them worthier of her time than he was? No, she'd had a child and she was a mother. But that was enough. The rest of her life would be spent in the service of other families—helping them stay together. With great mistakes came great penance.

The church was a half-hour drive from the ranch, and it sat on the crest of a hill in a pool of golden morning sunlight. The church property was squeezed between two fields, young green wheat rippling in the breeze on either side. It was beautiful, and from their vantage point, she could see the pickup trucks turning into the church property and parallel parking along the fence.

"I have to say," Casey observed. "You have a gift for reassuring people. One conversation with you, and I felt a whole lot better."

"That's about as close as I'm going to get to you telling me you approve of my profession, isn't it?" she asked with a low laugh.

"Yup." But he shot her a grin. "You're a good woman, Ember. I'm glad I've gotten to know you a bit…properly."

They turned into the parking area in front of the church. Casey parallel parked next to another truck and turned off the engine. He sucked in a deep breath, then glanced over his shoulder at the babies.

"Am I crazy to think I can do this, Ember?" Casey asked softly.

"No, you're daring," she replied. "And there's a difference."

Casey smiled, then nodded. "All right, then. Here's the plan. We each carry a baby, I'll take the diaper bag and we see how we all fare through church."

The next few minutes were spent getting the babies out of the truck and wrapped in blankets against the chilly morning air. People stopped to say hi and peek into the blankets to get a better look at the babies, so their progress to the church was relatively slow. When they finally got inside and got seated, Ember adjusted Will in her arms, then glanced over at Casey.

"I think you'll be okay," she said. "There are several women who would be more than happy to hold babies for you."

"Yeah… I hadn't thought of that, exactly," he said.

"Mr. Vern said you've got a village," she noted. "I'm inclined to agree."

"It might take a village," Casey said, and for a moment his gaze warmed and enveloped her. "But we three guys here need more than a village. We need a mom in the family."

Her heart clenched in her chest, and for just a moment, she had an image in her mind of what it might be like to be that mom. A handsome husband, two adorable boys, living out in the Montana wilds… But she pushed it back. No, that wasn't for her—he hadn't even hinted at that! He needed a wife and a mom for these boys, and he'd find a woman worthy of them all.

To save her from answering, a lady at the front began to play the first chords of a hymn, and everyone started to settle and put their attention into the service that was about to begin. A family… That thought tugged at a part of her that she'd thought was dormant. She didn't want to be the mother to other children. She didn't deserve it…so why was she feeling that yearning when she looked over at Casey and the babies?

Lord, provide Casey with the wife he wants so badly, she prayed silently. *And don't let me want what isn't for me…*

It couldn't be her, but that didn't mean he didn't deserve someone really wonderful. So did Will and Wyatt. They all deserved a woman far less broken than she was.

* * *

The service went smoothly enough. The babies slept through most of it, waking up for bottles once. Sitting in that pew next to Ember was an oddly endearing experience. She was petite next to him. Her personality made her seem bigger than she was, and looking down at her, watching her smooth one ivory hand over Will's downy head, he'd felt his heart swell. She was beautiful and gentle, and while she seemed to try to hold herself back somehow with the babies, there were moments like that one in church when he could see the tenderness in her gentle touch. But she'd made it clear that she didn't want to be a mom.

What should that little detail even matter? She was a Reed come to buy the ranch out from under him, but in a little country church with babies in their arms, those facts felt cloudy and distant. He'd convinced himself that his trip to church would be more of his promised tour of the area, not a quiet moment as the sermon washed over them, her shoulder pressed warmly up against his as the babies slumbered in their arms.

The pastor spoke about new beginnings. He and his wife were moving on to a new church shortly, and there would be a proper farewell service midweek. Today, however, they'd have a big potluck in the church basement, and everyone would have a chance to say how much they appreciated this pastoral family.

Except when the service ended and Casey turned his phone back on, there was a text waiting for him from Bert. There was a new calf to be bottle-fed that had been rejected by its mother. Casey would have to go over to make the final call on whether or not the calf would need a vet. A ranch didn't stop running on

Sundays, and Casey couldn't leave all the work to the remaining workers. Bert said his wife had a respite worker with her elderly mother at the moment, and she could watch the babies for a few minutes if Casey would just say the word, so Casey answered the text in the affirmative, grateful for the offer.

"Ember, I've got to head back. There's a calf that needs tending. Bert's wife can stay with the babies for a few minutes. Did you…want to come with me and see the barn? Or stay longer here at church? Should be a good potluck…"

"I'll come," she said, and he felt a funny wave of comfort at those words. He shouldn't be getting attached—she was certainly not a permanent fixture in his life. If anything, she'd be the one to push him out of this little church he loved so well and into another county with another ranch to be managed.

And yet having her at his side was strangely comforting. He'd need to get his head on straight with that.

The sky was overcast as they stepped outside. Two hours had made all the difference, and now the day looked gray and chilly. The cloud cover hung low, and Casey was confident they'd have rain before the day was through. Good. The land needed it. There were vast fields of crops and pasture depending on spring showers, and he'd never been one to be depressed by rain. Rain meant farming success, and the promise of a downpour always cheered him right up.

They got the babies back into their car seats and within a few minutes they were heading down the highway again, back toward the ranch.

"Does Mr. Vern normally attend that church?" Ember asked.

"Yeah, normally," he said. "He must be wanting some time to himself, what with all the hard stuff with Linda lately."

"He came back late last night. It was past midnight." She looked out the window, and her face was shielded from his view. "I was already in bed, but I wasn't sleeping. I think he wanted to be alone anyway. He made it pretty clear before that he didn't want to talk about it."

"It's a tough time for him," Casey said.

"I know." She glanced back and cast him a small smile. "And not every man likes to talk. That's okay. I can slide into work mode pretty easily, and I don't take it personally. It's the therapist in me that wants to help. That's all."

Work mode. Yesterday, that talk they'd had that had made him feel so much better about raising two boys on his own had felt more personal. She had her own pain, too, and she'd been opening up to him little by little. It didn't feel like a professional divide between them. But maybe that was just him not used to therapists and the like. This mess of feelings—that was all part of the job for her.

"So how do you separate that out?" he asked. "The work mode versus, I don't know, like, real human connections."

"When I'm working, people come to me for my unbiased perspective," she replied.

"Like I did," he clarified.

"I suppose."

"And when it's more personal?" He glanced over at her, and he realized he cared about this answer a whole lot.

"They want my bias," she said with a small smile, and he couldn't help but smile back.

"Okay." Casey turned onto the road leading up to the barn. Professional—that was what this was, and he had to remember that. Even if having this woman so close the last couple of days was starting to make those lines feel blurred. It was the childcare—that was the great equalizer, it seemed. Add to that, she was beautiful in the most disarming way...

Casey stopped at his house, where Bert's wife, Fiona, was already waiting. She happily took over with the boys and waved Casey back out of the house.

"The sooner you sort things out, the sooner you'll be back," she said with a good-natured smile. "Don't worry about me. I'm happy to snuggle some babies."

Casey got back into the truck where Ember was waiting, and the gravel crunched under his tires as he turned again out onto the road that led down toward the cow barn.

"I haven't given you a tour of the cow barn yet," Casey said as he steered around a pothole and stepped on the gas.

"That's true..." She glanced over at him. "Not that it will matter much for my purposes."

Casey was silent for a moment, but something had occurred to him...something he could choose to conceal. That would be more convenient for his own goals. Still, he'd promised honesty. "There might be some better-preserved records in Cascade County," he said. "I knew a guy who was researching his ancestry, and he found some information that way. No promise that they'll have what you're looking for, but it's something."

She brightened. "Thanks, Casey. I'll try that tomorrow morning. I can send some emails and make a few calls. Sunday should be rest...technically."

"Yeah, not for a cowboy." He shot her a smile.

"What happened with the calf?" she asked after a beat of silence.

"I'm not sure. We've got an orphaned calf is all I know."

She was more relaxed out here in the truck, away from everyone else. She seemed different alone with him, and he wondered if she shared his affinity for quiet and for the fresh afternoon air coming in through the partially opened window. Was it petty of him to hope that her search in Cascade would end up in his favor? He was supposed to be on the side of truth, not just on his own side.

They drove in silence the rest of the way, and Casey pulled to a stop outside the barn then put the truck into Park. They both got out, and Casey glanced up at the sky. A chilly wind was blowing, and the clouds were moving at a pretty good rate overhead. Maybe that rain would come faster than he'd thought.

"So this barn was built about twelve years ago," Casey said as he came around the truck and met her on the other side. "The original barn that was in this location was storm damaged from a particularly nasty winter, and Mr. Vern took the opportunity to completely replace it that summer. It was pretty costly, but it was going to be worth it in the long run."

Ember looked at the barn, then around herself at the surrounding land. There was more he could tell her, but he decided against it. She wasn't interested in cow barns, and he knew it. She wanted to find her connection to her own family history, and a barn wasn't part of that. Besides, they were here for a calf.

"Let's head in," he said.

He matched his pace to Ember's, slowing down a bit as they headed toward the barn. She was little compared to him, and that floral scent from the truck still whispered close by. He pulled open the barn door and she stepped in ahead of him.

The long, low barn was the place where sick cattle came to be treated or separated from the herd for whatever reason. This was also the makeshift nursery for motherless calves. Casey led the way past an aisle of supplies neatly stacked on shelves, and down to a section of stalls that were set aside for the calves. The ranch hand Greg Stein was crouched in the nearest stall next to a tiny calf covered in a blanket.

"Hey, Mr. Courtright," Greg said, rising to his feet. "I found it in the south field—the mother had twins and abandoned this one. We tried to reintroduce them, but she wouldn't take it back. Bert said to wait for you."

"How bad is it?" Casey asked, moving into the stall next to the cowboy and squatting down to take a closer look.

"Hard to tell. I was just cleaning it off and was going to try to warm it up," Greg replied. He seemed to take notice of Ember just then, because he added, "Ma'am."

"This is Ember Reed," Casey said, unwilling to give more explanation than that. "Ember, this is Greg Stein, one of our ranch hands who's been here for about four years now."

"Pleasure, ma'am." Greg leaned over and shook her hand. "We're working half-crew, so if you don't mind, I'll get back out to my duties, sir."

"Absolutely. I'll take it from here," Casey said, and he watched as the young man headed back out. Casey angled his head, inviting Ember into the stall.

"Poor thing," Ember said, sinking down to her haunches next to the calf.

"I'm going to go grab a new blanket and get some calf formula to get this little guy started," Casey said, standing back up.

"Can I help?" She looked up, clear gaze meeting his. He hadn't expected that. He'd figured she'd want to stand back and watch.

"Uh—" He shrugged, then smiled tentatively. "Yeah, if you want to. Why don't you use that blanket and wipe the calf down. The mother didn't clean him off properly, and he's cold."

Without another word, Ember turned to do as he'd asked, rubbing the blanket over the calf's head and shoulders, murmuring reassuringly as she worked. Her movements were confident and gentle, and if Casey didn't know differently, he'd have thought she'd worked with cattle all her life.

"Thanks," he murmured, more to himself than to her. He watched her for a moment longer before he pulled his mind back to the task at hand and headed down the aisle of supplies to fetch a clean bottle and some formula powder to mix up. That calf would be hungry and weak, and it needed strength if it was going to pull through this.

When he returned with a new blanket and the freshly mixed bottle, he found the calf clean. He handed Ember the new blanket.

"We need to keep him warm," Casey said. "So just cover him up to keep his body heat in."

Ember settled the blanket over the calf, and Casey handed her the bottle. "You want to do the honors? Same idea as in the house, just bigger."

Ember chuckled and took the bottle of formula. The calf could smell milk and nuzzled toward the nipple. Casey leaned down, grabbing the end of the bottle to get it up at the right angle for the calf to drink. Except when he knelt down to help Ember, he found his face right next to hers, the warmth of her cheek emanating against his rough stubble. She smelled sweet, and he had to physically stop himself from putting an arm around her in that position—it would only feel natural. But that wasn't his place, and while she didn't seem to notice how close he was, he stayed motionless for a moment while the calf got its rhythm.

"You have it?" he asked, his voice low, and she nodded, so he pulled back, cool air rushing between them once more. "You're a natural."

"It's just a helpless little thing," she said.

Yeah, so were the twins back at the house, but she hadn't engaged with them like this—wholeheartedly. So what was the difference?

Milk foamed around the calf's slurping mouth and dripped down its chin.

"You're a person who connects with animals, then," he said.

"I always liked the idea of a hobby farm," she said, then glanced up at him. "And I know that probably sets your teeth on edge."

"A little," he admitted with a low laugh.

"You never did tell me what drew you to this line of work," she said, her eyes still on the calf as it drank.

"I was born on a ranch," he said. "I told you that. It's what I know."

"Yeah, but plenty of country boys end up in the city," she replied.

He shrugged. "True. I like it. I—" He wasn't sure he had the words to encompass what this meant to him. "It's like it's a part of me somehow. When I'm on horseback, everything else melts away. When I look at a herd, I'm already looking ahead to what needs to be done...but it's more than that. Cattle are soothing. A contented herd almost purrs."

Ember looked up at him; her expression softened. "And you're willing to work another man's land in order to work with cattle."

"Yeah. It's not the ideal, but it's better than nothing, isn't it?"

"But you won't work for me."

Casey let out a soft laugh. "No, ma'am, I won't."

She smiled ruefully and dropped her gaze. "I like that."

"That I won't work for you?" He squinted at her, unsure what to make of this woman.

"No, you refusing to work for me is annoying, because from what I can see, you're the best around, and I want only the best," she said. "What I like is being called 'ma'am.'"

"Aren't you called 'doc' or anything like that at work?" he asked.

"It's not the same. 'Ma'am' is...based on nothing more than the fact that I'm a woman. It's...reassuring somehow."

"That's country manners," he replied.

She was silent, and Casey sank down onto an upturned bucket, watching as the calf drained the last of the bottle. Ember pulled the nipple out of the calf's grasping mouth and passed it over.

"So what drew you to therapy?" he said.

"I want to help." She smoothed a hand over the calf's head. "After I started college I hit a really rough patch. I struggled with depression, and there was a therapist on campus who helped me through it all. I was young, scared, heartbroken, orphaned—"

"You had a father."

"I had a biological father, not someone who loved me like Mom had." She sighed. "That therapist helped me to straighten it all out in my head. If it hadn't been for her, I would have partied away my life, looking for comfort in all the wrong places. She's the one who said that faith could be a safe place in all the chaos. I was angry at God then, and she wasn't even a Christian therapist. She was just helping me find my footing again, and that one comment she made stuck. I thought about it for a week or two, and one morning after a rough night, her words seemed exceptionally true and I gave my heart to God. I needed to look higher. And when I'd made it out of my own hard time, I realized that I wanted to do that for other people—help them sort it all out and point them higher."

"I can't imagine how hard that must have been," Casey said quietly. "You were pretty young."

"It was tough." She nodded. "But even in our darkest valleys, there is always something brighter on the other side. There has to be, or how could we keep going? Sometimes we just need another person to believe it strongly enough that we get swept along in their current of hope."

"I guess that's faith," he said. "Believing, even though you've been marching around those walls for what feels like an eternity."

"I guess it is." She smiled up at him.

Except Ember was the one standing between him and the one thing he'd been longing for—independence, land of his own. She was vulnerable, beautiful, and just as impossible to get around as stone walls. So why did he have to feel this strange mixture of emotions when he was with her? She was part of the problem, and he just couldn't bring himself to resent her anymore. But whether or not he found her likable, beautiful, or endearing in her own way, she'd walk away with this ranch if she wanted it.

Absolutely nothing was simple with Ember.

Chapter Seven

Ember watched as Casey settled the calf with another, older calf. They curled up together in new hay, and Ember and Casey leaned against the rails, watching them.

"The calf will be okay, won't it?" Ember asked.

"The odds are pretty good," Casey said. "A belly full of milk goes a long way."

Funny how attached she could get to a calf in half an hour. But the little guy looked like he was settling in comfortably in the hay, and she sent up a silent prayer that he'd thrive. It was tough to picture now. He was so small, so dependent.

"That's a hard start without a mother," she said softly.

"Oh, but he'll get attention and bottles full of milk. He'll be part of a rotation of bottle-fed calves, so the ranch hands will come by every three hours and give him another bottle."

"So this is normal," she said.

"There's always three or four," Casey said. "Come on. Let's let the little guy rest."

Ember could see why Casey loved this ranch so much. It was more than charm—the place had a certain amount of heart to it. And almost all of the employees would be left out of work if she fulfilled her goal. Change was never easy, and a success for one person always meant a failure for another...or for a whole ranch worth of employees.

That thought sat heavily for Ember as they drove back to Casey's house.

Casey breathed out a long sigh as he turned off the truck, and Ember eyed him curiously. He looked worn and tired, but also eager.

"You've missed the babies," she said.

He looked over at her, lifted his cowboy hat off his head and ran his fingers through his hair. "I guess I have."

The first few fat drops of rain started to fall, each landing on the windshield with a wet thwack, and Ember leaned forward to look up at the darkening sky.

"Let's get in there before the skies open, shall we?" he said.

"Excellent idea," she said with a grin, and they both pushed open their doors.

Ember had farther to run than Casey did, but he waited for her at his side of the truck all the same. Then they made the dash to the side door together. He turned the knob and pushed open the door, then stood back to let her inside first. As they erupted into the house, there was a flash of lightning and the rain came down in sheets. Ember shivered and Casey swung the door shut. It was then that she heard the reedy wails of the babies crying in unison.

"You're back," Bert said, coming into the kitchen

with a baby propped up on his shoulder and a panicked look on his lined face. "They just won't settle. Fiona's finishing with Wyatt's diaper, but—"

Fiona came into the kitchen at that moment with Wyatt in her arms. She looked less stressed than her husband, and she held Wyatt close to her cheek, making a soft shushing sound next to him that didn't seem to be helping much.

"Thanks for standing in," Casey said, taking Will from Bert's arms. "Much appreciated."

Fiona handed Wyatt over, and the older couple exchanged a look of unmitigated relief.

"I'm glad you're back," Fiona said, putting a gentle hand on Ember's shoulder as she tried to adjust the wailing infant in her arms. "Too much change, I'll warrant. They just need a quiet evening with their daddy. Will's settling down already."

And he was—Will's cries had softened into whimpers, and as Casey swung the baby from side to side, he seemed to be winding down.

"Thanks again," Casey said, raising his voice over the babies' sobs. "I'm really grateful. My aunt will be here to help me out middle of next week, so there's an end in sight for you, Bert."

"It's not a problem," Bert said with a grin, but all the same, he put a hand in the center of his wife's back and propelled her forward toward the door. "Have a good night!"

When Bert and Fiona had left, Ember's attention turned to Wyatt, who hadn't calmed in the least. She jiggled him a couple of times, her heart filling with misgiving.

"Just rock him," Casey said, still swinging Will in that perfect arc that seemed to be working for the baby.

"I am!" Ember jiggled Wyatt a few more times, then started rocking back and forth, but Wyatt wasn't having it. And in Ember's heart, she saw a tiny calf without a mother, and deeper down still was the memory of her own tiny boy, who had cried for her so desperately as another woman took him away.

"He wants his *mother*—that isn't me," she said, tears rising up inside her.

"Well, she isn't an option anymore, is she?" Casey shot back. "She's gone! So hold that baby like you mean it!"

Like she meant it. She'd been holding herself back whenever she cradled either baby, and she'd been repressing all those instincts on purpose. She was trying to stem the flood of memories of her own little boy, and the harder she tried, the more vivid he was in her heart.

She'd never named him, had let his adoptive parents have the honor—that was supposed to make it easier. But it hadn't been. They hadn't let her be a part of anything…and nothing of her had gone with her son to his new home, nothing but his memories that would have faded eventually, and she couldn't help but wonder if a part deep inside him would always be wounded, wondering why his mother gave him up.

"No—" Ember's voice quivered as she swallowed back tears, but Casey's arms were already full, and she couldn't very well just put the sobbing baby into the cradle and walk away. He needed something, and she wasn't enough—she couldn't be.

"Ember, just—" Casey didn't seem to know how

to put it into words, but Ember knew what it would take to quiet this child—it would take her whole heart.

So with a prayer for strength, she pulled Wyatt in close against her cheek, shut her eyes to the room around her and rocked him with all the love that had lain dormant in her heart this long, long decade. She rocked him the way she wished she could have rocked her own little boy, soothing away that anguished cry as they'd walked away with him, cooing over him as if his tiny heart hadn't been searching for her in that swarm of strangers.

And as she rocked, her tears flowed, and Wyatt calmed. He sucked in a few ragged breaths and snuggled against her neck. That was what he'd needed—for her to open herself up, empty herself out.

"Ember…" Casey's voice was low and concerned, and she opened her eyes to find him looking into her face. He put a hand out and touched her cheek with the back of one finger.

"Sorry," she whispered. "It's—" She swallowed.

"What happened to you?" he whispered. "And don't tell me it's nothing, because I'm no fool."

Ember had never told anyone else about her son. He'd been her heavy secret, and giving him up had been her deepest heartbreak. She looked down at Wyatt, now stilled and soothed in her arms, then back up at Casey.

Casey stepped closer still and pushed her hair away from her face, wiping a tear off her cheekbone with the same movement. Those brown eyes were locked on hers, and she sucked in a ragged breath.

"I gave up a baby boy for adoption ten years ago, and

it's been hard lately," she admitted softly. It sounded so…ordinary.

"So that's why…" He nodded a couple of times. Had she not hidden her pain as successfully as she thought?

"I've been trying to just set it aside for now," she said, wiping a tear from her cheek with the flat of her palm. "I'm sorry. I didn't want to do this. I knew I'd have to deal with it, but I wanted to wait until I was back home…and alone. So… I'm sorry. I'm not supposed to be melting down here—"

"Hey, it's okay." He met her gaze tenderly. "You weren't ready to give him up, were you?"

"I thought I was." Ember licked her lips and looked down at little Wyatt, whose eyes had drooped shut. Her arms were already feeling tired, and she looked up at Casey helplessly.

"Come sit," Casey said. "It'll be more comfortable."

Ember followed Casey into the living room, and they sank down into the couch, side by side. For a few beats they sat in silence, and then Casey said quietly, "So what happened?"

"You don't have to do this," she said, her voice raspy with unshed tears.

"I'm asking as…I don't know…a friend, I guess."

Ember looked over at Casey. "Are we friends?" she asked hesitantly.

"I thought so. We seem to have gotten there. Aren't we?"

Ember let the silence flood around her once more, and then she sucked in a breath. "I was seventeen when my mother died, and I didn't know how to grieve. I was stuck being angry—I was so mad that my mother had left me. It wasn't her fault, but I wasn't ready to be alone without her yet…" Ember's voice trembled, and she cleared her throat. "So instead of feeling it all, I tried to avoid it. While she was dying, I was busy running away from the heartbreak I wasn't ready to feel. I drank. I partied. I did whatever I could to numb the pain."

"And your father?" Casey prodded.

"My father told me that if I didn't straighten up, I'd never see another penny from him. I don't blame him. Obviously, I was out of control." Ember looked down at the slumbering infant, then smoothed his hair with her fingertips. "So I pulled myself together enough to pass muster. I started college—my dad got me in— and I tried to just put my childhood behind me. I actually thought that was possible! I'd kept up the partying through college, and one night… I don't remember anything from the party, but the next morning, I was pretty sure I did some things I regretted. Some friends took pictures, and I was—" She looked away, feeling the heat rise in her cheeks, even after all this time. "It doesn't matter. Suffice it to say, while I didn't know it yet, I'd conceived my son that night, and I had no idea who the father was."

"How old were you?" he asked.

"Twenty. Old enough to know better," she said, then shook her head. "I had to tell my father, and he suggested—rather strongly—that I give the baby up for adoption. I wasn't in any position to be properly supporting myself, much less a child. I had no idea who the father was, so I couldn't get help from him. I was halfway through my first degree, and if I dropped out and raised my son on my own, I'd have been a poor, single mom, just like my own mother. I was scared, and I thought that if I could only adjust my thinking and know from the start that I was giving the baby up that I wouldn't get attached."

"Did it work?" he asked softly.

"I thought so… I chose a family—a pastor and his wife who were childless. They were good people, and I knew they'd love him and raise him well. I brought them to doctor's appointments and everything. But then when he was born, it felt different," she said, and the memory of her little boy's squished, red face rose up in her heart so forcefully that it felt like a punch. "His adoptive mother talked to me a little bit. She said they were naming him Steven. And that name was all wrong…my son wasn't a Steven, but I had no say. I forced myself to sign the papers, thinking that if I just got over that hurdle, it wouldn't hurt so badly. Then she asked if she could hold him. I tried to be strong, and I said yes. She took him from my arms." Ember closed her eyes, steadying her breath. "I'll never forget that cry… I dream of it still."

She felt Casey's hand close over hers, and she looked over at him to find his eyes misted with tears.

"They say it'll get easier, that you'll go on with your life… Except it never got easier for me." She shook her head faintly. "I can't call my son Steven. I still haven't named him in my heart, but he isn't a Steven. He's just my baby."

And her heart still ached for him, as did her arms. She wouldn't be complete again, because he was gone, and he was no longer a baby, either. Time had swept him away along with that adoptive family.

"I'm sorry," Casey murmured, and his grip on her

hand tightened. It was comforting, and she was glad for the contact with him, rooting her to the present.

"Ironically, I thought that searching out this property would be a welcome distraction from it all." She smiled bitterly.

"And then I show up with the twins." He finished the thought for her.

She didn't answer, but they both knew it was true.

"Is this why you don't want children of your own?" Casey asked.

"Yes." She nodded, her control coming back. "I didn't pray about it—not in earnest—before I gave my son up. I just closed my eyes and did it, and it was the biggest mistake of my life, trying to please a father who never really loved me in order to keep my financial security. Adoption is a good and right decision for so many people, but not for me."

Ember looked over at the big cowboy, wondering what he was thinking just then, but he didn't say anything, just looked down at her hand in his.

"You don't stop being a mother when you give your child away," she went on, hoping he could understand this. "I carry him in my heart, and I pray for him constantly. He has a birth mother who loves him more than he'll ever know."

"You should forgive yourself," Casey said quietly.

"Have you given up a child?" she asked, meeting his gaze painfully.

"No." He swallowed.

"It isn't about forgiving myself," she said softly. "It's about living with myself. Two different things."

"Is it?" Casey shook his head. "It might feel different to you, but I'm pretty sure they're the same thing."

"You can't understand," she said.

"I can try." He released her hand and put his arm up across the couch, his rough hand close to her face, and she wished she could lean into him, feel his calloused palm against her cheek. Comfort… But longing for physical comfort could be a dangerous thing, and she'd learned that lesson young.

"When I gave up my son, I knew I couldn't ever be a mother to another child. Adopted or biological—how could I tell my son I gave him away, but I kept another child? No, I knew when I gave him up that I was closing the door on future motherhood, and I'd focus my life on the good I could do for others."

"Penance?" he asked quietly.

"Of sorts," she agreed.

"I'm sorry if I made all of this that much harder," Casey said, looking down at the infant in his arms. "If I'd known what you were going through, I obviously would never have asked you to help me with the babies—"

"But you didn't know." She shook her head. "I'm fine, Casey. I really am."

And ultimately, Ember *was* fine. She was educated, she had a career, an avenue where she could help others through their difficult times, and she was that much more sympathetic to the shortcomings of her patients because she had been in their shoes and made choices that she'd later regretted, too. Her past weakness made her a better therapist today.

"Do you need to stop this? Helping with the babies, I mean," Casey asked.

"I can't avoid infants forever," she replied. "You need help, and my mission here hasn't changed. I know

I had a bit of a meltdown today, but I'm really okay. I promise."

"For the record, it sounds to me like you were young and confused, and did what you thought was the right thing for you and your baby," Casey said. He leaned forward and used the back of one finger to brush a tendril of hair away from her cheek, his touch lingering there. She let her eyes flutter shut and leaned her cheek against his warm hand. But when she opened her eyes and looked into his face, she saw no judgment there. His voice was low and warm. "It was forgivable, Ember."

And while she knew that anything was forgivable in a contrite heart, forgiveness wouldn't erase the consequences of her actions. Forgiveness wouldn't return the child she'd given away. This wasn't about absolution so much as grief. And a mother never stopped being a mother to her child.

"Thanks," she said with a sad smile. "But I'm okay."

And she was. She was sad, she was living with deep regret and she had more hard-won wisdom than any other thirty-year-old woman she knew. But she was okay, because she was still in God's hands.

Outside, the rain continued to fall, puddles forming on the gravel road and the patchy grass beside it. While she wished she could just lean into Casey's strong arms and rest there awhile, she knew better. No man could fix this. Even a sweet man like Casey with those dark, gentle eyes and that stubborn streak that kept him good. He'd be an excellent father to these little boys. God was providing for these tiny orphans, and she could see that plainly.

But Casey Courtright wasn't the answer to her

prayers or her tears in the dark. Right now, all she could do was carry on. There would be light ahead eventually.

Chapter Eight

That night, Ember crawled into bed with the two heavy quilts on top of her, and she dreamed of her son as she so often did. She heard his infant cries and her dream-self was determined to find him. She would not hold herself back—not this time! She went down a hallway, opening door after door; she kept searching and searching, his cry so close. But whenever she tried to call out, her voice wouldn't respond, and the baby's sobs seemed to come from every direction at once. She woke up sweating and gasping for breath.

"Steven…" she choked out. He wasn't Steven to her…but it was the name he'd be called throughout his life. He wasn't a tiny infant anymore—he'd be a ten-year-old now, a tall boy with his own opinions.

Did he look like her? If she were to see him again, would she see her own features in his? But that was a dangerous line of thought, because she *wouldn't* see him again. She had agreed to stay away. Unless he searched her out when he was an adult, that had been their last goodbye. Not every adopted child wanted to meet his birth mother. She might still yearn for him, but that didn't mean he wouldn't be perfectly happy and fulfilled in the life he'd been given.

Ember swung her legs over the edge of her bed and sat there for a few minutes, pulling herself out of the dream and reaching out in prayer.

"Father, take the dreams away," she murmured. "And wherever he is, protect my son. Bless him. Provide for him. Pull close to him and let him feel loved."

The nightmares had been getting worse lately, and caring for Casey's charges wasn't helping matters. This visit to Vern Acres wasn't supposed to be such a drawn-out affair, either. She should be finished with this task already. Finding her family's land and starting up her own enterprise on it was going to fill her heart and squeeze out that aching sense of loss. Life *had* to move on.

She'd meant to wait until Monday morning, but last night she'd found the Cascade County Historical Society and had gone ahead and sent them an email. She'd gotten an automated reply saying that someone would be in touch at their earliest convenience, and she was hopeful that there might be some sort of information that could guide her. *Something.*

But everything seemed to be spinning out of her control, including her ability to keep her personal issues private. She pulled a quilt over her legs again, shivering against the night air. Her mind went back to yesterday when she'd said far too much. She hadn't meant to speak to him about her son. She kept telling herself it was only the timing—she'd kind of melted down in front of him, after all, and he'd deserved an explanation. But it was more than that. Casey was warm, strong, resolute and oddly comforting. She'd told him because she'd *wanted* to. What did that mean?

She'd kept her secret locked away these last ten years, opening her heart for no one. And having revealed her deepest regret left her feeling vulnerable in a whole new way.

Ember shivered, tugging the quilts back up over her shoulders. It was time to refocus her priorities. When the sun rose, she would see how close she could get to Harper Creek and see what was out there. She might be hoping for proof that wouldn't even exist anymore, but at least she'd be able to see it all firsthand. She had to get moving on this—or she'd lose herself here.

And she fell back into a fitful slumber.

That morning, Ember awoke feeling less than rested. It had been a rough night, and the thought of helping with the infants this morning was too much to face. She could fall in love with those baby boys a little too easily.

When she ambled into the kitchen that morning, Mr. Vern had just come back in from his early chores. He poured himself a mug of coffee, and another for Ember.

"So how much of the ranch have you managed to see?" Mr. Vern asked as they sipped their brew together.

"I've seen a few fields, both barns, some silos—" Ember swallowed a scalding sip. "What I really want to see is Milk River, though."

"It's a ways out," Mr. Vern said. "You mind if I ask why seeing it is so important?"

"My great-great-grandmother's journal mentioned the names of some creeks off the river in the area of their homestead. Those old names don't exist anymore, but there is a Harper Creek. My family name is Harper. I'm wondering if it's possible that my family settled by that creek. I know it's a long shot."

"How would you even know if you did find the right land?" Mr. Vern asked.

"My great-great-great-grandfather brought a single red brick from New York State when they came out to settle here in Montana. He built it into the front of their fireplace as a reminder of where they came from. I don't know if anything would even remain of an original structure, but if it did…"

"You're right. It's a very long shot. And I hate to be the bearer of bad news, but there is also this…" Mr. Vern rose from the table and sauntered out of the room. He came back a moment later with a map that he unfolded and stretched over the tabletop.

"This is an older map," Mr. Vern said, "and you'll see Harper Creek isn't on it. That creek was renamed for a mayor in the seventies."

Ember sighed. Another dead end. Except she still wanted to see it…get close enough. Who knew? Maybe she'd recognize something there on a heart level. That was crazy, and she knew it, but when her mother used to tell her those family stories, she used to think that if she could just stand on the soil that her family had homesteaded, she'd feel them there…their memories, the family connection. She was a grown woman now and wasn't the superstitious type, but still…

"—but if you want to see Milk River, get an idea of the area," Mr. Vern went on, "there's a service road that will take you all the way up there. It brings you a little east of this area you were looking at on the map, but it's something."

"Really?" Ember looked at the older man in interest. "How far is the drive?"

"An hour, maybe less," Mr. Vern said, leaning back over the map. "There—this road here. You follow it up past the cow barn, and it circles east, so it's not quite in the same direction you're wanting to go, but it does bring you right close to Milk River here—" he jabbed a finger at the map "—and you can get a good look. That's as close as you get without going on horseback."

"That sounds doable!" Ember grinned. She wasn't sure what she hoped to see…or feel. But she needed to at least lay her eyes on the river, get close enough to touch it.

"I can't take you today, myself. I'm going back to the nursing home to see my wife. They're saying that she needs to be transferred to a different facility that can give her more services." He sighed. "I could get Casey to give you a ride."

Casey—no, he was turning out to be a little *too* comforting lately.

"No, no." Ember shook her head quickly. "Casey's a busy man, and I don't need him to chauffeur me everywhere. If it's just a matter of following a service road, I'm perfectly capable of doing that."

"Your GPS won't work on those service roads," Mr. Vern warned.

"Understood."

"And there's no cell service out there."

Ember shot him a grin. "I'll survive. It's just a road. Would you be able to lend me a vehicle so I could drive up there and take a look?"

"Can you drive stick?" Mr. Vern asked, raising an eyebrow.

"Sure can."

"Then you can take the red truck." He went to a wooden board covered in hooks and key rings, and pulled down a set of keys. "You sure you don't want that chauffeur? Casey would be happy to take you up there, I'm certain."

"I'd rather do it alone," she said.

"Suit yourself. Don't wander too far from your vehicle, and keep a sharp eye out. The wolves are hungry this time of year. They tend to leave people alone, but I'd still keep pretty close to the truck, regardless."

"I'll be fine," she said with a smile. "I appreciate this, Mr. Vern. I want to get closer to the river. I don't know what I expect to see, but—"

"Understood. Drive safe. I won't be here this morning, so when you get back, if you could just put the keys on top of the sun visor, I'd be much obliged." Mr. Vern gave her a nod, and Ember felt a weight lift off her shoulders.

Freedom, at last. She'd been praying all this time that God would show her what she needed to see out here on Vern Ranch. Maybe this was the land she was meant to buy, and maybe it wasn't. But it was hard to listen for God's voice when always surrounded by people. If God was going to show her something, she had a feeling He'd do it when she was alone and listening.

She was so ready for some solitude that she felt like skipping at the thought of getting out on the road by herself.

Guide me, Lord, she prayed. *Help me to know if this land is my family's or not.*

Casey spent the morning checking on some new calves out in the south field. The cows hid their babies, so they could be hard to find sometimes, but there were nine new calves in the herd as of this morning—at least that he could see. Ember hadn't come to take care of the babies today. She'd called him to let him know that she was taking a drive south to see the river, and Casey didn't have much say in that. She had the boss's permission and seemed intent on going.

"You sure?" he'd asked. "It's pretty rugged out there."

"I'm positive, Casey. I'm just letting you know where I'll be." There'd been a finality in her tone that told him she wasn't interested in being mollycoddled.

One of the homeschooled girls from church came for the morning to do some babysitting, for which Casey was eternally grateful, and he'd headed off for his workday, doing his best not to worry about Ember.

She'd drive on down to the river, check things out and drive back. There wasn't much to it. He'd called twice to check on her—he was the manager on this ranch, after all, and her safety was his business—but there was no cell service out there, so it was no surprise that she hadn't picked up. Except, she'd been gone now for five hours, and Casey couldn't help that stab of worry.

His cell phone rang, and Casey dug it out of his pocket, glanced at the number and picked up the call.

"Mr. Vern," Casey said, punching the speaker button and dropping the phone to his lap. "What can I do for you?"

"Have you heard from Miss Reed yet?" the older man asked. "I just got back, and I don't see the truck. Is she still out there?"

"It looks like," Casey said. "I'm starting to get concerned. She might have had a flat or something. I was thinking of going out there to check on her."

"That's a good idea," Mr. Vern agreed. "If you'd drive on out and get tabs on her, I'd feel better."

"Will do, sir. I'll head in that direction now."

Casey pulled to the side of the road and dialed his house number. The babysitter picked up, her voice hushed.

"Are they sleeping?" Casey asked.

"Yes, finally," the girl replied. "Diapers changed, and they're due for a bottle soon, but I don't want to wake them up. What do you think, Mr. Courtright?"

"Wake them up one at a time to feed them," he said. "Or you'll have two hungry babies at once."

"Okay, I'll do that," she answered.

"I'm going to be a bit later than I thought, Jane. Are you okay to stay another hour or two?"

"Sure thing," she responded. "It's no problem. I'll just call my parents and tell them."

"Thanks," he said. "I'll be back as soon as I can."

Casey pulled a U-turn and headed back down the service road in the direction of the cow barn. It was a good forty-minute drive to the river if he stepped on it, so he had time to think. Normally, he liked the solitude, but today, he found himself frustrated and antsy. Having Ember on this ranch was turning into a real irritant. He couldn't seem to stop thinking about her. She wasn't quite so self-sufficient as she seemed to think, and whether she liked it or not, he was worried about her. He wanted to keep her safe.

Last night, she'd opened up, and it was only having infants in their arms that had stopped him from pulling her close. It would have been instinct—and not the kind of instinct he had with every other woman in his life. Ember was different. She was tugging at his defenses in the most infuriating way, because while she was the one standing between him and his life's goal of owning his own land, he also found himself drawn to her.

"You're an idiot," he muttered to himself.

Ember's emotional situation was her business…but he did care, even though he knew he shouldn't. In fact, he cared too much.

Ember's story about the baby she'd been talked into giving up… That had stuck in his heart like a shard of glass. He couldn't quite forget it. If Ember hadn't lost her own mother so young, she might have had someone on her side who could have given her better advice. Or if her mother agreed that adoption was the best choice, maybe she would have been able to help her make her peace with it all. A little support might have gone a long way.

Casey had lost his mother young, too. He'd been fifteen, and she'd drowned in a boating accident one summer. So he knew what it felt like to be motherless when he still needed a mom. The difference for him was that he'd still had his father. They'd pulled tight and moved forward together.

If this land truly had belonged to Ember's family, he knew what that would mean to her. But this land would mean the world to him and his dad, too. Will and Wyatt might grow up right here. Casey had grown up on a family ranch, and there was no experience that could compare. That was something he might be able to give these boys—a decent childhood.

For the next forty minutes, Casey drove down that long, straight road, dust billowing up behind him. Finally, ahead at the side of the road where it took a sharp turn, Casey could see the red truck. He slowed down as he approached, unsure if he should be relieved or not, because it was empty. His truck rumbled to a stop behind the other vehicle and he turned off the engine. Outside, all was silent and still. Casey got out of his truck, and a brisk wind whipped around him.

"Ember!" he called.

The wind whisked his voice away, and he grabbed a rifle from the rack at the back of his cab and slammed the door shut. Where was she?

He hooked a boot up on his truck's bumper and stood up straight, getting a higher view over the terrain. From that vantage point, he could make out the slope of the land going down toward the river. He looked in both directions.

Harper Creek was west from here, and Casey shaded his eyes as he looked in that direction. He could make out some movement down by the water farther down the river. A flash of purple, and relief flooded over him. She was fine. He'd been worried for nothing—and that forty-minute drive was for nothing, too. He had work of his own to do and a teen babysitter doing overtime so that he could come out here and make sure she was okay. He should be piping mad.

What did it say that he was this glad to see her again when fetching her was such a wild inconvenience?

Chapter Nine

Ember sank lower on her haunches, holding her breath as the beaver swam silently closer, dark shining eyes looking at her above the water.

The narrow creek that led off the river had been dammed up by the animals, and she'd been watching them for some time now.

Beaver Creek—that had been one of the creeks, hadn't it? There was no saying this was the same creek because beavers could certainly move locations, but she couldn't help but wonder…

She was looking for proof, and she likely would never find it. But what would be proof enough for her to buy this land? How much did she need to be certain of the purchase in her own heart, even if not in her head?

"Ember!"

Ember startled. The beavers all disappeared with soft plops as they skirted beneath the water, and she twisted to look behind her. She knew that voice, and then Casey was marching through the brush toward her, a gun over one shoulder and his eyes blazing in annoyance.

"Casey—" She pushed herself to her feet.

"What are you doing out here?" He stopped to scan the brush and trees, that glittering gaze coming back to land on her.

"What am I doing?" Her own annoyance was rising now. "I'm looking at the land I'd like to buy. I'm trying to get a closer look at Milk River. That is why I'm on this ranch to begin with, isn't it?"

"No, that much is understood," he retorted. "The part I have trouble with is that you've been gone for almost six hours now."

"I drove up the road farther, came back, looked around on both sides of the river and discovered the beavers here. I've been...busy."

"You should have let me drive you," he said. "You crossed the river?" He closed his eyes, seeming to be looking for some calm.

Let him drive her? No, that was the exact thing she'd been avoiding. Instead, she'd had time alone—a precious, silent commune with her Maker. And she'd had some time to pull herself back together. Being thrust into the company of strangers as she navigated newborn babies, a ranch and her own ambitions left very little time for her to sort out her own feelings. She was the kind of person who needed solitude for that.

"I didn't want company," she replied honestly. "I needed to be alone for a while."

Casey's annoyance seemed to slip, and he dropped his gaze, glaring down at his boots for a few beats before he looked to the side, his dark gaze moving over the trees and toward the burbling creek. She'd offended him, and that wasn't her intention, either. It wasn't his fault she'd been a weepy mess.

"I'm embarrassed, Casey," she said tightly, "if I have to spell it out for you. I said too much last night. None of that was your business, and I—I should have kept my mouth shut and I'm regretting that."

"Regretting having opened up," he clarified, that intense gaze snapping back to her face once more.

"Yes."

"Thanks." His tone was dry.

"You think last night was appropriate?" she asked with a short laugh. "Because it wasn't! You asked me a question professionally, and I…I totally crossed lines there. My history, my personal issues—none of those matter. They're mine to deal with. So I should be apologizing to you—"

"You aren't my therapist!" he shot back, cutting off her words. "Do you see a counseling office out here?"

"Isn't that the point?" she retorted. "To have an inviting environment? Apparently, it works rather well on me, too."

"You aren't my therapist, Ember," he repeated. This time, his voice was a low rumble. "Let's keep that clear. I don't need a therapist, nor do I want one. When I talk to you—if I open up—it isn't about professional boundaries."

"You asked me as a professional," she countered.

"Okay, I did—" He shook his head. "*Once.* I phrased it badly. What can I say? I'm telling you now that you can let all those boundaries go around me. You aren't my therapist and never will be. Neither will you ever be my boss. I think I've been clear about that one, too. Things between us aren't 'professional' because I haven't hired you and you haven't hired me. You opened up because you felt safe enough to do it. So quit running away up your ivory tower."

"I'm not running away," she responded, turning back toward the creek. "I'm taking care of my own business."

"Well, your safety is *my* business," he shot back. "And I had to drive forty minutes to come find you because Mr. Vern was worried."

"Mr. Vern was?" She looked back at Casey over her shoulder, and his cheeks flushed slightly. She felt the smile tickle her lips. "It wasn't Mr. Vern who was worried, was it? It was you."

"It was both of us. You have no gun," he said. "And you're a bit far from the truck, aren't you?"

Ember looked toward her vehicle and realized it was hidden behind trees. She sighed. "I may have strayed a little far. But I'm obviously fine."

"Obviously," he said dryly. "And that couldn't possibly have changed at any moment."

"So maybe I should be glad you found me," she admitted.

Ember turned back toward the creek and squatted back down. The beavers had disappeared—all was silent except for the twitter of birds and the rush of water from Milk River a few yards off. She scanned the dam—a bulging tangle of sticks and branches that seemed to hold together by a will of their own.

"There is a story in that old journal about beavers damming up a creek and turning the garden into a marsh." Ember sighed. "They had to move the garden. It was easier than moving the beavers. But the potato crop was ruined. They nearly starved that winter."

Twigs cracked under Casey's boots as he came up

to her side. "This land might be beautiful, but it's not easy. It never has been."

"I don't need it to be. My family survived because they learned as they went," Ember said. "My great-great-great-grandfather did everything from building their log house to trapping meat to feed the family. That winter when they didn't have enough food, he fed the family on rabbits and deer. When they lost their cow to wolves, they trapped beaver and traded their pelts for another cow the next summer, and then built a new barn right next to the house so they could protect it better."

She'd been raised on those stories—the tales of ancestors from long ago who had passed down their grit and determination to the generations that would come after. If they could survive blinding blizzards that lasted for days…if they could keep their family warm by burning cow dung and stopping up the cracks in their house with mud and hay…if they could break up that hard prairie earth and make it grow vegetables…then what about the rest of them? What could they survive?

"Those journals are priceless," he said.

"They are. They tell us what we're capable of. They homesteaded on the prairies before it was tame. And they made it."

Casey was silent for a moment. "Your mom sounds like she was pretty tough, too."

"She was." Ember smiled sadly. "But she was pragmatic, too. She always told me not to make her mistakes—never get pregnant before I was ready. She worked her fingers to the bone to provide for me, but she also reminded me that my great-great-great-grandmother who survived so much on the Montana prairies died in childbirth having her ninth baby. She was only forty-three."

"Was that a warning?" Casey asked.

"Yes," she replied, her mind going back to her mother's earnest face—tired and lined from long hours at work. They used to talk together late at night when Mom got back from her cleaning shift at the high-rise office building and after Ember had finished her homework. They'd sit in the kitchen together, eating a quick dinner, and that was when Mom was the most honest, when she had the least energy to keep things bright for Ember's sake.

"Mom always said that we can survive nearly anything for a while, but eventually life catches up. She didn't want me to be foolhardy."

"Like coming out here on your own?" he asked with a small smile.

"I was thinking about my son—what she would have advised if she'd been around," she replied softly. Ember glanced over at Casey, gauging his interest, worried that he might be judging her. His dark eyes were pinned on her, but she saw sympathy there, nothing else.

"Would she have suggested you raise him on your own?" Casey asked.

"I didn't think so at the time," Ember said, her throat thickening with rising emotion. "I thought she'd say the same thing my dad was saying—that the best thing I could do would be to give him a life with someone else. I wasn't ready to be a mom yet. She always told me not to make her mistake—to wait until I was ready. She said it was harder than I needed to know, and she wanted better for me. So when I found out I was pregnant—" Ember could hear the hoarseness in her own voice, and she took a beat to swallow. "She would have been really disappointed in me."

"And your father knew that." Casey's voice hardened.

"I don't think so," she replied with a sigh. "He just had no intention of supporting a single mother. He wanted me to make something of myself. It seemed like the smart choice."

"If you had it to do over again?" he asked, and a breeze picked up, chilly, wet air winding through the woods, and Ember wrapped her arms around her body and found herself stepping instinctively closer to Casey just as he did the same. He didn't retreat, though, and instead put his warm palms on her upper arms.

"I'd keep my son," she said, her voice nearly choked. "I'd do whatever it took."

"Why don't you hate your father for putting you in that position?" Casey asked, shaking his head.

"Because it wasn't his fault. My choices were on me. I was an adult and I could have told my father to get out of my life and leave me alone. I could have done what my mother did and worked my heart out to provide for my child."

But she'd believed what everyone told her—life didn't have to be that hard. Life could be sweet and simple. She could get another chance to build a life she was proud of, and this mistake could all just melt into the past. They were wrong, of course, but she'd believed what she'd wanted to believe.

"Twenty isn't all that grown up," Casey said gruffly, and he moved a tendril of hair away from her eyes. She looked up at him, her breath catching in her throat. Those dark eyes were entrancing, and she should look away, break this moment, but she didn't want to. She'd been so afraid to let her secret out for fear of being judged for it, that to have this man understand… But he was being too lenient on her.

"What were you doing at twenty?" she asked softly.

"I was a cattleman."

"See?" she murmured. "Quite grown-up."

"I sure thought so," he said with a rueful smile. "I'd imagine you did, too. But I wasn't. I was outspoken and I thought I knew it all… But no, I wasn't grown-up, and I would live to be proved wrong on a whole lot."

"Me, too," she said, and another finger of cold wind worked its way between them. She shivered, and Casey tugged her just a little bit closer, so close that his lips hovered over hers. He wrapped his arms around her securely, and his eyes locked on hers.

"What are you doing?" she whispered.

"I don't know," he murmured back.

"I thought I was the bad guy…"

"I forgot," he said ruefully, and his gaze flickered upward, just for a moment, and then he froze, the moment evaporating around them. He slowly pulled his arms from her waist, and those dark, direct eyes were locked on something behind her.

"What?" she breathed, whipping around, and she saw a wolf several paces ahead of them on a rise, crouched down and teeth bared. The animal was huge—so much bigger than she'd imagined them to be. This was no "dog," but a feral beast who was looking at them as its next meal. Her heart hammered hard in her throat, and she sent up a wordless, panicked prayer for help.

Casey's eyes never left the wolf, and he didn't even seem to hurry as he pulled the gun from the strap that held it on his shoulder and reached into a pocket, coming out with two red-tipped shells. He cracked the shotgun open and dropped the shells into place.

"Don't move, Ember," he murmured, his voice low and quiet. "Don't…move…"

Casey snapped the gun closed, aiming it over Ember's shoulder—directly at the wolf. Ember was trembling, her breath coming in ragged gasps as she stared at the massive, shaggy predator. Its fur hung heavy and patchy, still thin from a long, cold winter. This wolf was hungry, and for a split second, Casey felt the entire forest slow down to a crawl.

The wind shifted a tendril of Ember's hair as if in slow motion, and Casey felt the barrel of the gun snap together into the loaded position in his palm. His muscles knew the movements, so he didn't even need to think about them.

He locked eyes with the wolf, watching as its golden gaze narrowed almost imperceptibly. Then the wolf's shoulder twitched.

"Drop—" Casey ordered, his voice hollow, and Ember obediently crouched down just as Casey pulled the trigger. There was a deafening bang and the wolf dropped where it stood, the huge, shaggy beast slumping to the ground.

Casey let out a pent-up breath, then quickly surveyed the trees around them. He had another shell in that gun, and if there were more wolves—

Ember tried to stagger to her feet, but she pitched to the side on her way up, her hands going to her ears protectively. That was why he'd told her to duck—he could have made the shot past her, but the sound of the gunshot right by her ear would have deafened her. Casey raced out a hand to catch her and managed only to graze the soft material of her jacket before she stumbled away.

He let her go. Casey's eyes were scanning the woods, the river, the trees—looking for more hungry eyes and shaggy gray coats. Because where there was one wolf, there were always more.

"Ember—" he barked, and as he spun in her direction, he saw her walking unsteadily toward the creek. Then she lost her footing and plunged into the icy water. Casey darted forward and caught her outstretched arm as she sank down with a cry.

He grabbed her under one arm and hauled her back onto dry land, but as she came out, she cried out again and nearly collapsed as her weight hit one foot. She'd hurt herself—that was plain as day, and his heart pounded in his ears even as he spun back around to keep up his surveillance.

"Let's get back to the truck," he snapped. He didn't mean to sound as harsh as his voice came out. He *did* care about the fear written all over her face, and the gasp of pain as he dragged her forward, forcing her to keep walking, even though her knee buckled underneath her. But they didn't have time to linger. The wolves spotted weakness and it piqued their instinct to attack. They needed to get back to a vehicle fast.

Ember tried to limp after him, but she wasn't going to be fast enough. There was a blur of gray across the river, and another one beyond that. He had one shell loaded, and it wasn't going to be enough to take on a pack of hungry wolves.

"God protect us!" he whispered aloud, then swept

an arm underneath Ember's legs and whipped her up into his strong grasp.

Staggering forward, he hurried through the marshy undergrowth up to firmer ground, but as he ran he could hear the howls of wolves behind them. They only had seconds—if that!—and he knew it. Running away only encouraged these predators.

His breath was like fire in his chest as he dashed as fast as he could run up the rocky incline toward the trucks. He could make out the blaze of their paint through the trees—so close, yet so far, and then as if by instinct alone, he dropped Ember to the ground, stepped in front of her and spread his arms wide, bellowing his loudest roar.

Two wolves stopped in their tracks only a few yards away from them, low growls coming from deep in their throats.

"Father, save us—" Ember whispered, and his own heart echoed her prayer with every beat.

"Hey!" Casey shouted. "Back off! Hey!"

The wolves took a tentative step back, and Casey whipped the gun from where it hung on his shoulder, pointed it at the closest wolf and pulled the trigger. With a thunderous bang, the animal dropped dead, and the other turned and sprinted into the forest.

There was still no time to waste—Casey put an arm around Ember's waist and hauled her forward as they scrambled the last few yards to the truck. Casey pulled open the passenger-side door and shoved Ember inside first. She cried out in pain—again something he noticed and definitely cared about, but he still didn't have time to soften his approach. Then he headed around to the driver's side, keeping his eyes peeled for more movement in the trees.

He was out of shells—at least loaded shells—and he was vulnerable out there. The pack might just cut their losses, but wolves were smart, too. They grieved a loss to their pack, and they avenged it.

The driver's-side door opened as Ember pushed it for him, and he jumped into the cab, slamming the door shut behind him. He was breathing hard, and he turned the key, the engine rumbling to life.

"You okay?" He turned toward Ember and she looked as white as paper, her lips trembling. "You aren't… Ember, you're hurt—"

"My ankle—it twisted when I fell in the water, and—" She squeezed her eyes shut. Casey had no idea how bad the injury was, but by the look of her, she needed some medical attention—the sooner the better.

"I'm going to drive us a few miles away from here, and then I'm going to take a look at that ankle," he said. "I'm going to need to get out of the truck to help you, and I'd rather not do that with wolves at my back."

She nodded mutely, her eyes still shut, and Casey slammed the truck into Reverse, turned around and then started down the road once more the way he'd come, leaving the red truck behind them. He'd send a couple of guys out tomorrow to pick up the truck—with a warning to stay clear of the trees.

The truck bounced over a bump, and he grimaced in sympathy as Ember gasped in pain.

"I'm sorry," he said. "I'm being careful—I promise."

"I'm okay—" she breathed.

"Liar," he retorted. "But you will be. Don't worry. I've got you."

As he drove toward the welcoming expanse of open field, he was filled with relief. Wolves would have a hard time ambushing him from pasture, and the more minutes that ticked by, and the closer they got to the settlement, the safer they were. Once the trees were about five minutes behind them, Casey let up on the gas and pulled to the side of the road.

He had a first-aid kit in the truck—every ranch vehicle had one—and he grabbed it from behind the seat before he jumped out and headed around to her. He opened her door and put a hand on her knee.

"Okay, I'm going to lift your foot out of the truck, and we're going to get your shoe off," he said.

Ember nodded, and Casey put a supportive hand under her shoe as he brought her leg out so he could see how bad it was. Her jeans were wet through, as was her shoe. She was already shivering with cold. He pulled a knife out of his belt, slicing through the laces of her shoe in one flick of his wrist, and he pulled the shoe off, then rolled off her sodden sock.

"I'm going to owe you for those laces," he said wryly, his fingers moving expertly over the puffy, swollen flesh of her ankle. Her skin was damp and chilled, but there was heat pulsing from deeper in her flesh. "Move your toes."

She winced but she managed to move her big toe, so it wasn't a break. But it was a very bad sprain, and the pain must be excruciating. He dropped the first-aid kit in her lap so that he could keep a hand under that foot. If he let go, she'd probably pass out from the pain.

"I need you to get out the tensor bandage," he said. "I don't think it's broken, but it'll hurt a whole lot less once I get this wrapped."

Ember fumbled with the zipper, but opened the kit and handed him the bandage roll. He worked quickly, starting at her pale toes and moving up her already bruising foot. He wrapped tightly, keeping her ankle supported until he'd finished the job. Then he gently put her foot down on the floor of the truck.

"There," he said.

"Thank you." Her voice was soft, and when he looked up at her, he found blue eyes fixed on him with a look of overwhelming gratitude. "You saved my life, Casey."

"Oh, hey…" He wasn't sure how to answer her, so he shrugged. "And my own, right?"

She smiled, then shook her head. "Play it off all you want, Casey Courtright, but you just faced down a pack of wolves for me today."

And I'd do it again in a heartbeat, he realized ruefully.

"Next time you want to come out here, wait for me and let me give you the ride," he said gruffly and slammed her door shut, heading around to the driver's side once more. When he pulled himself back into the driver's seat, he leaned over and grabbed her seat belt, pulled the belt out long and clicked it into place before he let go. The emergency was past, and the last thing he needed was another one.

"I'm sorry," she said. "You're right—that was my fault. I was stupid and naive, and—"

"Hey, it's over," he said, clicking his own seat belt into place. He looked over at her, her blond waves tumbling down over her shoulders, the color so pale that it almost matched the whiteness of her skin. Her lips were pale, too, the only color in her face right now that of her glittering blue eyes that were misting with unshed tears.

Casey reached over and caught her hand in his. He lifted her fingers to his lips and kissed them, keeping his lips against her skin longer than he needed to. It helped stabilize him a little bit. He'd almost lost her today, and his heart was still catching up with that. "I'm just glad you're okay."

He lowered her hand and put the truck back into Drive. Then he pulled back onto the gravel road, his heartbeat still not quite slowing down to normal.

There were dangers out here that Ember hadn't even thought of. And she wanted to let the land go wild and bring a bunch of city folk onto the property! Maybe after they risked life and limb they'd walk away from here with a little bit of perspective, he thought bitterly, her idea of a therapy center sounding crazier than ever.

And her idea to come out here alone was even crazier.

He was angry, he realized, because it was easier than processing the rest of his pounding emotions. And his anger wasn't about the land being ranched anymore, or even about her father—in this moment, it was about her safety.

If she'd gone out there and gotten herself killed, he'd have lost something that was only just awakening in his heart. What it was, he couldn't say, but he knew he'd carry that loss with him for the rest of his life.

"Let's get you back to my place, and we'll get you dried off and warmed up. That'll help matters, too. Just make sure you bring me with you the next time you go exploring," he said, glancing over at her.

"I will."

"Promise me," he pressed. This mattered. It was her safety on the line.

"I promise." And those blue eyes met his and his heart stuttered in his chest. Whatever he was feeling for her was a very bad idea. He just wished he had a choice in the matter.

Chapter Ten

An hour later, Ember sat in the La-Z-Boy chair, pulled up next to the wood-burning stove in Casey's living room. Orange flames glowed behind the glass, and heat pumped pleasantly against her aching foot. Her jeans were still damp, but warm now, and steadily drying. The fear and pain from her recent adventure were melting away as she sat in that chair.

Thank You for protecting us, she prayed in her heart. *I could have died out there. If Casey had been a few minutes later, or if the wolves hadn't stopped when he confronted them... Father, You protected us!*

The babies were sleeping in the matching cradles, and from the kitchen, she could hear Casey clattering away putting together a sandwich for her. That stubborn cowboy was still taking care of her, and she felt so grateful for it all that she could almost cry.

It was only now sinking in how close she'd come to meeting her Maker. The memory of those white fangs bared, the fur standing up on end, the sparkling, hungry eyes... A shudder ran down her spine. If Casey hadn't swept her up in his arms the way he had and carried her most of the way to the truck, if he hadn't faced the wolves himself, roaring back at them as if he could take on a pack of wolves with his own ferocious desire to protect her—

Casey had saved her life, and he'd proved today what he was made of. He was a brave, good man who would lay it all on the line for a stranger who was going to buy this land out from under him.

Can I do it? Ember leaned her head back against the chair and breathed out a sigh. Unless she was certain this land was the site of the Harper homestead, she couldn't go through with buying it. One ranch was as good as another for her professional purposes. There would be other options. Unless this was the Harper land, the place where all those family stories had taken place—then she would have a claim on this land and she wouldn't be able to walk away.

She'd gotten an email back from the Cascade County Historical Society and found it on her phone when they returned to the ranch. While they didn't have any information for her directly, they did have a website with scanned early photos from the area. Most were undated and about half had some names attached. But if she wanted to go through the website, she might find some familiar people, or images of landmarks her ancestor had described. For what it was worth...

She'd asked God to show her something out there at Milk River, and she'd seen the rugged beauty of nature and felt a strange connection to this land...right up until they'd been hunted by a pack of hungry wolves. What did it mean? Was this land for her, or was God showing her how foolhardy she was being over this? She wished the message were clear!

"Is the aspirin helping?" Casey asked, coming back into the room with a fat sandwich on a plate.

"It took the edge off the pain," she said. "Thanks."

Casey handed her the sandwich, and she adjusted herself in her chair, sitting up a little taller so she could eat.

"Aren't you going to have one?" she asked. The sandwich—turkey, lettuce, tomato and cheese—was sliced diagonally in half, and she took half then handed him the plate. "Come on. We were in that adventure together."

Casey accepted the plate with a small smile. "All right. I do make one good sandwich."

He raised his half in a sort of salute and took a bite. Ember took a bite, too, her teeth sinking into soft white bread with a tangy crunch of pickle. It was delicious, and she finished half of it before pausing to look up. She found his eyes locked on her, his expression oddly grim.

"You're a surprise," she said, meeting his gaze.

"Yeah? How so?"

"I've never had a man pick me up and run me to safety before," she said.

"A guy does what he has to do," he said, a smile flickering at his lips. "Getting you into my arms wasn't such a hardship."

"You're flirting," she said with a low laugh.

"Cut me some slack. We could have died out there."

"What would you have done if the wolves hadn't backed down?" she asked.

"Died?" He laughed softly. "You aren't supposed to run—that piques their instinct to chase. But I had to get you closer to the truck. When I turned on them, I did what you're supposed to do—face them, make noise, look big."

"And shoot," she added.

"If you can. I had one shell left—we got out of there alive because of God. I didn't have enough time to reload."

Ember believed that, too. Their prayers had been answered, but she'd still watched that man stare death in the face in order to protect her. If he'd left her behind, he could have gotten to safety much more easily—but somehow she knew that had never been an option for him.

Casey put a hand on her wrapped ankle. "How much does it hurt?"

She shrugged weakly. "It'll heal."

"I guess you got a real, up close view of this land today," he said.

"It's not what I thought." She heaved a sigh. "I figured I could handle it—whatever dangers might lurk on this land. I didn't expect…that."

"Yeah, well…there are ways to deal with the dangers, but they never actually go away. We're just careful. We know what dangers lurk, and we're prepared. I know it's overwhelming right now, and telling you that you could still do this goes directly against my best interests at the moment, but it's the truth. You could learn all of this, too—figure out how to really be prepared."

"You think I could actually turn this land into my therapy center?" she asked dubiously.

"I'm saying you could survive it," he said with a short laugh.

Casey pulled a stool up and sat down, his hand still resting protectively on her ankle.

"I didn't expect you to say that," she said softly.

"I'm an honest guy," he said, and she saw the sadness in his gaze as he said it.

"I'm not buying this land unless I'm sure it's the Harper homestead," she said quietly. "I'm no country woman. I don't know how to deal with all the dangers of land this wild. It would be foolhardy for me to even try without a really good reason—"

"I'm not trying to scare you," he said earnestly. "I need you to know that."

"Those wolves—that was scare enough," she replied with a rueful shake of her head. "I'm not blaming you, Casey. You can't help it if you were right."

Casey's phone buzzed in his pocket and he froze. He pressed his lips together into a line, then rose to his feet, pulling the phone from his pocket. Whatever he'd been about to say, he'd decided against it.

"Hey, Bert," Casey said into his phone, and he walked a few steps away. "Yeah. Okay... Where?"

Ember finished her sandwich, and as she chewed the last bite, she leaned forward to gingerly touch her bandaged ankle. It was a bad sprain, but the tight bandage was helping to support her joint. Casey was a good emergency medic, and if he could soften up toward her, he'd be a good manager of what remained of the ranch if she did buy the place. She was fast realizing that there would be few others she could possibly trust the way she trusted this man, and if she did open her therapy center here, she would feel safer, more confident, maybe even happier with him at her side.

Except he'd been clear that she'd never be his boss. If she bought this land then he wouldn't be staying.

Whatever they were starting to feel between them—it couldn't last.

"I'll be there soon," Casey said, then hung up the call. He looked over at her, his expression conflicted.

"What's going on?" she asked.

"There's a cow having trouble delivering in the south pasture. The cowboys doing patrol don't have the equipment with them to help the cow, so I'll have to head on out there. I don't want to just leave you like this, and the babies—" He glanced toward the sleeping infants in the cradles.

Ember gingerly lifted her foot to the ground. She could stand up if she put her weight on the good leg only.

"It's a sprained ankle. I'm not exactly out of commission," she said.

"Hold on a second." Casey disappeared up the stairs, and she could hear his footfalls overhead. There was a rustle against the floor, a thump, and then his steps came back down the stairs once more. He emerged into the living room holding a single crutch.

"You just had that hanging around?" she asked with a soft laugh.

"What can I say—I'm ready for emergencies. It's part of the job."

"That will help enormously." She accepted the crutch, and he held out a hand, helping her to stand on her good foot. Then he adjusted the crutch for her height.

"There you go." He sounded satisfied, and with the crutch's support, she did feel a lot more mobile. "Would you watch the babies while I go take care of this?"

"Sure."

"Are you sure you'll be okay? I know this is really

hard for you, and I don't want to add to it. I probably never should have asked for you to help out with the babies to begin with, but—"

"Casey." She put a hand on his arm. "I'll be fine."

Casey looked down at her—and she was struck again by just how big this man was. Tall, broad, strong, and those dark eyes were fixed on her with an expression so complex she couldn't read it. But she didn't need to read his thoughts to know what kind of man he was. All she knew was that in this room with him, she felt warmer and safer than she had in her life.

"If I'd lost you out there—" He clamped his mouth shut, as if biting off the words.

"But you didn't," she said.

"I'm just saying—" He didn't want to say it, whatever it was. She could tell by the battle on his face. "I've known you a week. This is a strange circumstance— what with the babies and now the wolves... We're not exactly in an ordinary situation here."

"I agree," she said softly, but his eyes were still locked on hers.

"So why does this feel like more?" he asked, his voice a low rumble.

It *did* feel like more. It felt like something deep and undeniable was developing between them, despite the fact that she could never be a mother to his sons, and he could never support her as she fulfilled her promises to God. They were stuck, but her heart kept stretching anyway. Her stubborn, stubborn heart that wouldn't let go, even when it was for the best.

Like with her own son that her heart yearned toward, even in her sleep. She'd given him up. He had another family. He wouldn't even remember her! But her heart wouldn't stop and she dreamed of his infant cries anyway.

"Go and do your job. I have it under control here," she said with more surety than she felt.

She glanced toward the babies, still sleeping deeply. Will's tongue was stuck out, and Wyatt was sucking rhythmically on a soother.

"I'm going to regret this," he said with a sigh. Then he dipped his head down and caught her lips with his. His lips were soft and warm, and they moved over hers with confidence. Her eyes fluttered shut, and she felt like the room evaporated around them, and all that was left was him and her and the whisper of his breath against her face. He slid his arms around her waist, tugging her closer against him. Then his hand moved up to her cheek as he pulled back and looked down into her eyes.

For the first time since this whole drama with the wolves had unfolded, she felt a rush of comfort, as if in this tall cowboy's arms, she'd come home.

"How inappropriate was that?" he murmured.

"Wildly," she breathed.

"Thought so. I'll kick myself for it later, but I couldn't leave the house without doing that just once—" He swallowed, closed his eyes for a moment, then stepped away from her. Cool air rushed between them, and Ember wished she could close that distance once more and just rest her cheek against his broad chest.

"I'll be back," he said and turned toward the kitchen and the door. She stood there, her lips still warm from his kiss and her heart hammering in her chest. All she wanted to do was run after him and have him do that all over again, but she couldn't run—and even if she could, she didn't dare. She knew as well as he did that there was no future between them…only these frustrating emotions.

Will squirmed in his sleep and let out a whimper. Ember used the crutch to hop over to the cradle, and she looked down at the sleeping baby. This was hard—opening up her heart for the sake of a defenseless baby, and then closing it up again for her own sake. It was like tearing open a wound every time she did it.

Ember couldn't be a mother to these children, no matter how sweet or deserving they might be. It would tear her heart out to do it. She'd shut the door on motherhood for good reason. She'd deemed her education and career important enough to hand her son to another woman. If it had been important enough once, it would have to be enough now.

Ember pulled the stool closer, sat down to give herself some proper balance and bent over the cradle to pick up the infant. Will snuggled against her chest, squirming to try to get closer. She sighed, leaning her cheek against the baby's downy head.

This ranch was a place of strangely deep emotion, and she couldn't help but wonder if that was because of some familial tie to the place calling her home.

Or was she only fooling herself? Because this ranch had ties to other families, too, and her emotions were tugging her toward one man right now—a man who needed a mother for his twins. She couldn't be that mother. She *could* be tough, strong, empathetic and staunchly determined to shepherd other people through their darkest times. She could be like the other women from the Harper family, standing tall and persevering. God had something He wanted her to do, and she'd felt

His hand in bringing her to Vern Acres. He would pay her back for everything she'd given up. She just had to hold on.

Casey tightened the saddle strap and led Soldier out of the barn. The only way to check out the situation in the south pasture was on horseback. He was going through the motions, but his mind wasn't on the job ahead of him. It was still back at the house with Ember—and that kiss.

It was dumb. He shouldn't have caved in to his desires like that. She was no country woman, and she had no desire to buy some land and raise cattle with him. He wanted to show those boys what hard work looked like, and how the day in, day out chores contributed to an industry that fed a nation. He wanted to raise those boys to say *Yes, sir* and *No, ma'am*. He wanted them to ride herd, earn the respect of the other men and stand by their word. He'd raise those kids right—just like he'd been raised, and like his dad before him.

Boys grew into men over time, regardless of where they did the growing, but life on a ranch did the best job of instilling time-honored values, in Casey's humble opinion. And Ember might like being called "ma'am," but she didn't understand the lifestyle that created those country manners. It wasn't just about using the words; it was about a sense of respect for women, a desire to live honestly and the humbleness that came from hard work. It started before dawn, and it ended when it ended—regardless of how many hours a man had been at it, or if the sun had already set.

Add to that, Ember didn't want to be a mother to any other children… Maybe that should have come first. They wanted different things, valued different things. Kissing her—he had no right to be crossing those lines with her.

And yet he wasn't sorry, and that frustrated him. He should feel bad about that—except that kiss had been honest. What he felt for her might be dumb as a bag of rocks, but that was how he felt when he looked at her. She was beautiful, wounded, more vulnerable than she liked to admit, and when he was next to her, all he could think about was if she was comfortable, and what she was thinking...

Casey put his foot into the stirrup and swung up into the saddle. He made a clucking sound with his mouth and pulled on the reins, guiding Soldier out of the barn.

Horseback was where he did his best thinking, so maybe this ride would do him good.

"Lord," he murmured aloud. "Take away whatever I'm feeling for her. I know she's all wrong for me. I don't even need help in seeing that. Just—take it away. Give me that peace that passes understanding."

God had always answered that prayer for him in the past. If something wasn't meant for him, he asked God to remove the desire for it. Like a woman he was interested in who wasn't a believer, or even some fancy truck he knew he couldn't actually afford. He'd pray for that peace, and he'd get it. Every time.

Except with Ember. He'd been praying for peace for days now, and God had gone silent.

Casey rode the rest of the way, the scenery passing him by without him giving it much notice as his mind gnawed over the problem. *He* was the problem—that was clear enough. Ember had come for one reason— to buy this ranch—and he'd been the one to overstep, pull her into his arms and kiss her. Given a chance to think that one over, she'd have every reason to be angry with him.

"Hey, boss!" Bert called as Casey rode up to where the old cowboy stood. The sun was lowering in the sky, shadows stretching long and languid. Cattle dotted the grassy field, grazing and chewing their cud. Casey spotted a few new calves since he'd last been out this way. He swung down from his horse and pulled the tools he'd brought with him out from the side bags. Then he patted the horse's rump, letting Soldier go graze with the cattle. They were close by Milk River, and Casey could see the glitter of the water from here. A creek snaked between two hills, copses of trees thrusting up from the banks.

"Right there." Bert nodded toward the cow. She was pacing, her head down as a ripple of contraction moved over her bulky middle. Her udder was leaking a steady drip of milk, and a pair of hooves poked out from beneath the tail. The baby was in the birth canal, but the mother looked exhausted. "Been like that for the last hour. No progression. I've tried getting in there to pull, but she won't let me close."

The cow shook her head, ear tags rattling, then hung her nose down again as another contraction hit.

"We're gonna have to get in there," Casey said. "That calf has to come out."

"Agreed," Bert replied. "But it'll take us both. I'll go around front and keep 'er occupied, and you see if you can get a hold of those hooves."

Bert and Casey had worked together on births for years now, and they had a well-oiled system. Cows had an instinct to go give birth alone, and they didn't welcome intervention, either, but this cow just might be tired enough to allow them to give a hand.

Casey had brought the calving chains with him—a device that settled over the cow's hips and attached to the hooves that were protruding. It gave the cowboy some leverage as he pulled the calf steadily out of the mother with every contraction. Closer to the barn, they'd put the cow in the head gate to keep her from getting spooked and trampling them, but he'd just have to be light on his feet tonight. Because there was no head gate available, and if this cow didn't get assistance, they'd lose them both.

"There've been wolves out—past the barn, on the east part of Milk River," Casey said, and Bert instinctively looked in that direction.

"How brave were they?" Bert asked.

"I shot two."

Bert's eyebrows went up, and he chewed the side of his cheek. "We'd better have a man with a gun patrolling tonight, or we'll lose the new calves."

"My thoughts, too," Casey agreed. "You ready?"

They moved toward the cow, and it took a few steps away from them. They approached again, and she did the same, moving steadily toward the river.

"Oh, no, you don't—" Casey got in front of the cow, cutting her off so she couldn't make more trouble for herself by getting too close to the water, and this time the cow stumbled to a stop as another contraction took over. For the next forty minutes, they assisted the cow in the delivery of the calf. It was a big male, and when it dropped to the ground, it didn't start breathing until Bert rubbed its chest with a handful of grass and Casey tickled its nostrils with another long stem. Finally, it pulled in a breath and they left the mother to clean up the baby.

They backed away to give the cow some space to bond with its calf, and Casey's boot hit something unexpectedly hard. Casey was on top of a small knoll, but instead of his boot connecting with dirt and grass, he'd hit sharp rock. He looked down, used the toe of his boot to work the soil away from the rock, and he frowned. That wasn't loose rubble. He kicked more, and Bert watched him curiously.

"What's the problem?" Bert asked.

"This—what is it?"

Bert came over and bent down, using his gnarled hands to pull weeds and soil away, then brushed the rocks clean.

"Looks like it's got some mortar between these rocks," Bert said, and between the two of them, they uncovered enough of the structure to recognize it. "That there's a chimney. Or what's left of it."

"Yeah. Looks like—"

Casey's heart sank. He'd sensed it the minute his boot hit it. There had been a cabin here, or a homestead, a long time ago. He looked around—it was an ideal spot, high enough to avoid flooding from the river and near a stretch of open plains. This had been a home once upon a time—possibly the homestead that Ember was searching for.

"You okay?" Bert asked, his lined face creasing with worry. "You look like you got bit by something."

"Help me dig down a bit. I want to see something…"

Bert gave him a funny look, but he complied, and they dug together for another couple of minutes. There wasn't much left in one piece, but as they uncovered more of the structure, at first he thought it was a chimney, and then he realized it was a hearth. Rock had been mortared together with some real skill, but then his gloved fingers hit something that felt different.

"What's that?" Bert asked when Casey brushed the soil away from it.

"A brick," he said hollowly.

"Huh."

A single brick mortared in with the rest of the rock. Ember had mentioned that...

"I know what this is," Casey said.

"Yeah?"

Casey slowly shook his head. "It's the end of my hopes for this place," he admitted, his chest constricting as the reality settled in.

He was an honest man, though, and a Christian. He wouldn't live a lie, and he'd given Ember his word that he'd help her find out the truth about this land. He'd just hoped that the truth would be more favorable to his position. How was it possible that this woman from the city with a rich daddy and a broken heart was the one with the rightful moral claim to this place?

This ranch wasn't rightfully his, either, but he'd been working this land long enough that he could have made it his, started out some new memories and put down his roots. He could have raised the boys here, and if he'd been able to see through his offer, his roots would have settled all the way down to the bedrock.

"Boss?" Bert pulled Casey out of his reverie. "You okay?"

"Yeah, Bert," he sighed. "But things are going to change around here."

"How so?" the older man asked with a frown.

"Miss Reed is going to buy this ranch."

"I figured that was why she was here," Bert said. "I'm sure she'll need a manager yet. And I'm due to retire here pretty soon. Fiona keeps asking me to hang up my spurs. We might not be rich, but we'll be okay."

"I'm not working for her," Casey said, his voice a growl.

"I know you're not crazy about the Reeds as a whole, but—"

"No, I can't work for her..." Casey sighed. "I'm feeling things for her that I shouldn't, and working with that woman isn't a possibility. I need a mother for those boys, and she's not it."

And there it was—the flood of certainty he'd been looking for on his ride over here, the knowledge he'd been avoiding when he was busy kissing the beautiful blonde in his living room. Ember Reed couldn't be the mother his boys needed. She couldn't be the wife to raise these kids with him. And while he could make his peace with her family background, he couldn't raise those boys at a therapy center. They needed land, cattle, chores and responsibility. He wanted to give them a proper ranch childhood...

There would have to be another woman to be the wife and mother they needed so badly. But it would have to wait until his heart had healed from this one...

Whatever he'd been hoping for—he needed to let those dreams go. Just because a man wanted something so badly he could taste it, that didn't mean it was part of God's plan. These weren't his walls. They'd been hers all along.

"Soldier," he called softly, and his horse nickered and sauntered in his direction. "Let's go, boy."

It was time to go back and face reality. He wouldn't be forgetting about that little detail again.

Chapter Eleven

The sun was setting outside the window. Ember held Wyatt in her arms, the baby looking at the glowing, partially blackened door of the woodstove in that cross-eyed new infant kind of way. Ember cradled the baby in one arm and used the crutch to sink back down onto the stool.

"Hey, you…" she said softly, and Wyatt lifted his head away from her shoulder, then let it drop down again. He had grown in the last week—she could tell by the way he fit in her arms. "How are you, little guy?"

Wyatt blinked up at her, big brown eyes fixed on her face searchingly. She smiled and smoothed a hand over his downy head. So small, so sweet…so easy to fall in love with.

"You deserve better than me, Wyatt," she said softly. "You remember that. You and your brother deserve only the best, and one day you'll have a mom of your very own."

Her throat tightened at that thought. One day, there would be a woman who'd be able to open her heart to these boys. She wouldn't be all emotionally battered like Ember was. She'd be whole and pure, and she'd be filled with good advice and endless hugs. She'd be the woman that Casey needed.

Ember sucked in a breath, trying to push back that stab of pain at the thought. She knew this little family of three deserved better, so why did it hurt so much to imagine what that better woman might be like? These boys needed a mom who could kiss away their pain, get them into line when they misbehaved and love their dad with all her heart. She'd be the center of that home, her love binding them all together.

"You deserve better, Wyatt," she whispered softly.

She'd missed out on all of this with her son—the snuggles, the diapers, the bottles. She'd given it away for the promise of a better future, believing that another woman would be better for her son, too.

It only occurred to her later that her father's advice that she give her baby up might have been coming from *his* experience. He'd known about Ember, had supported them with sporadic financial gifts and had otherwise stayed out of her life. He'd never seen her.

Hadn't that hurt him as a father? Hadn't there been some paternal part of him that had wondered about his little girl, worried about her, even? Because Ember thought about her son constantly, worried that he wouldn't know how much she'd loved him, that it would affect him later in life. She'd longed to see him again, just to know he was okay.

But her father seemed quite happy with how his life had gone without Ember there to complicate matters. He had a family already, wealth, respect in his community. He'd swept Ember aside like the mistake she had been.

The sound of boots on the step outside pulled Ember

out of her thoughts. She looked down at Wyatt, those big eyes still searching around him, taking in his little world. The door opened, and Casey came in, Bert on his heels.

"Hi," Ember said, forcing a smile. "How's the calf?"

"Fine and healthy," Casey replied, and those warm eyes met hers in a way that made her heart speed up just a little. Did he do that on purpose? "I brought Bert along to stay with the boys while I drop you back off at the house."

Bert could have dropped her off on his way home for the evening, but it seemed that Casey wanted the honor, and she felt a flood of warmth at the thought. She'd missed him, too, as inconvenient as that was. But opening her heart to her grief over her son also meant opening it up to everything else she might be feeling, and she wasn't able to simply push her emotions down.

"Let me just wash my hands," Bert said, heading for the kitchen sink, and Ember looked over at Casey. His dark eyes met hers, and she saw a strange mix of emotion there—so different from the tender longing in his eyes a few hours before when he'd kissed her. Had something changed? Or had he simply had time to think about it?

"How's the foot?" Casey asked quietly, coming up closer to keep his words private.

"Manageable," she said with a small smile.

"Could you ride?" he asked.

Ember eyed him uncertainly. "Right now?"

"No—tomorrow, maybe."

"Let's see how it feels tomorrow," she replied. "But I can guarantee you I won't be putting much weight on it."

Casey didn't say anything else, and when Bert dried his hands, Ember passed the baby over to his confident arms. Her heart tugged a little as she let the infant go. She was already attached to these little boys—how easily that happened. Bert gathered Wyatt up onto his shoulder.

"He's had his bottle and I changed his diaper half an hour ago. But normally after that bottle—" Ember began. Then she smiled sheepishly. "Sorry."

"Nothing to be sorry about," Bert replied. "And Will?"

"He's had his bottle, his diaper is changed and he's been out like a light since." So he'd wake up soon and want some entertaining.

"Sounds good," Bert said, then nodded to Casey. "Take your time, boss."

Ember got her jacket, and when Casey opened the door, she eyed the three steps with trepidation.

"Grab your crutch," Casey said, and when she did, he scooped her up into his arms. He smelled warm and musky, and her breath caught in her throat as he effortlessly carried her down the stairs, then put her down lightly once more.

"Now you're just showing off," she said with a low laugh as she caught her balance once more.

"Easier that way," he said with a wink, then pulled the house door shut behind him. "So how did it go with the boys?"

"Fine."

"I meant, how are *you*?" he said, his gaze catching hers.

"Better than I was before. There is something to

be said for just feeling your grief. It has less power that way."

"So they say." He looked away from her, scanning the scene for a moment, then bringing his gaze back to lock on to hers. "I could see us being in each other's lives, if you stuck around."

"But not as your therapist, and not as your boss," she said. She hopped over to the truck, and Casey pulled open the passenger-side door. She turned toward him, and he stood there looking down into her face, his eyes locking on to hers in that tender way again. His broad chest emanated heat in the cool evening, and she had to hold herself back from leaning into those strong arms.

"But I could be your friend," he said quietly.

"You're assuming I'm staying here," she said, sadness welling up inside her. "If I found the evidence I needed, I would. But I'm not buying this land without it. This isn't only about me and my feelings. My plans would affect a lot of other people…" Who was she fooling? She wasn't even thinking about the ranch hands who would be out of work or the wider community that wanted this to stay ranching land. "It would affect *you*, Casey. I don't like the thought of that."

Casey ran a finger down her cheek. Whatever it was about Casey that was so comforting and appealing, she'd have to sort out when she could be alone again. And while she couldn't just turn off whatever she was feeling, maybe she could wade through it and get to thinking rationally again.

"Hmm…" He didn't say anything else in response. Did he not believe her? Did he think she didn't care how he'd be affected?

"Casey, I'm serious—"

"I know you are," he said, and there was a flash of pain in those dark eyes. Then he dropped his gaze and pressed his lips together. "That's why I said I could be your friend. You're a good woman. I might think you're crazy, but you're deep-down good."

She smiled at that. "Crazy, am I?"

"I stand by that." He smiled ruefully. "I actually don't think I could stay away from you entirely. But I will stop kissing you in moments like this."

Ember felt a sink of disappointment at that. She didn't want him to turn off his feelings—even though it was best for both of them. But what did she expect? This wouldn't work between them, and she wasn't fooling herself about that.

"Okay," she said.

He pulled in another breath, then nodded. "Okay." He smiled into her eyes. "You want a hand up?"

"Sure." Casey put his hands on her waist and boosted her up into the passenger seat of the truck, and her stomach rippled at the sensation of his touch. He handed the crutch up to her, and then he slammed the door shut, leaving her in momentary silence as he circled around to the other side. She adjusted the crutch to fit more easily down by her feet and leaned her head back.

She'd pored over those grainy photos on her phone's internet browser while Casey had been gone, and there weren't any family photos that fit the descriptions from those journals. There were some unidentified pictures of wildly bearded men or somber women standing alone...but what did that help her? They could be anyone. It seemed there was no way to be certain whether this was her family's land or not. Maybe that was for the best. She didn't need to disrupt things here any longer. As soon as her car was ready at the shop, she'd leave Vern Acres and let Casey put his offer down on the ranch. He deserved it—he'd worked this land and maybe he was right that this county didn't need any more Reed influence.

Casey opened the driver's-side door and hopped up into the seat.

"So why do you want me to be able to ride?" Ember asked, glancing over at him.

"I want to show you something." He put the key in the ignition and the truck rumbled to life. "And we can only get there on horseback. That's one of the many complications of this place."

"What do you want to show me?" she asked, shooting him a curious look.

"You'll have to wait and see it yourself," he said with a small smile. "Words won't do it justice."

"And my ankle?" she said.

"I'll wait until it heals up enough to get you onto a horse."

Ember couldn't help the curiosity that bubbled up inside her, but when she looked over at Casey, his expression was resolute. She wasn't going to get anything out of him.

"Did you find something?" she pressed.

They pulled out onto that now-familiar gravel road and headed up toward the main house. Casey was obstinately silent, and she couldn't help but wonder if he'd stumbled across that proof she'd been searching for. Excitement simmered up within her.

Was this old ranch her home after all?

Chapter Twelve

That night, Casey sat in the kitchen, an untouched mug of tea on the table in front of him. His Bible lay open on the tabletop where he'd been rereading the story of Joshua and those walls.

"I'm sorry, Lord," he prayed. "I shouldn't have kissed her. That wasn't right—it doesn't matter what I feel for her. She's not mine to kiss."

He looked over at the cradles where the babies were sleeping peacefully. He was a dad now. He'd struggled with how he would handle all of this, but it had started to settle inside him. These boys were his responsibility, his God-given obligation. They were also his blessing and his joy. They needed him, and maybe he needed them just as much. Caring for these little guys was hard work—he couldn't deny that—but he'd fallen in love with them in the process.

"Make me a good father," he prayed, his voice choked. "Give me the wisdom I'm going to need to raise these boys right. Give me strength, and tenderness, and insight… Make me into the father that these kids need. And please, Lord, take away whatever it is that I'm feeling for Ember.

There is only so much a man can handle at one time, and I'm pretty sure I'm reaching my limit here..."

Once he showed Ember his discovery, she'd finalize her offer—and he'd need to figure out where he and the boys would go. Surely, God had something in mind for them. He'd given Casey a family, hadn't He? If that wasn't God moving in His own mysterious ways...

But Casey did need a woman in his life—a mother for those boys. He needed someone to stand by him, raise kids with him, wrestle with the hard stuff. He needed a woman who could help him teach those boys the country manners and the Christian morals. He needed a partner.

So what was he doing letting himself fall for Ember Reed? It was dumb—there was no way around it—but he also felt a little helpless when it came to his feelings for her. When he looked at Ember, a part of his heart he'd never known existed woke up.

Casey didn't sleep well that night. Telling Ember about that stone hearth with the single brick worked in that was by the river wouldn't be easy, because it would be a sort of goodbye to all of his hopes for this land, too. But at least he'd have some time alone with Ember and he could show her what she needed to see... alone, without an audience.

The next morning, he went to do his rounds after the ranch hands had completed the early chores. Bert stayed with the babies, and Casey called his aunt, just to make sure she was feeling well enough to start helping him out on a full-time basis the next week as they'd agreed. There were two baby boys who needed nurturing and love while he was working to provide for them, and his wayward heart was not the top priority. Those boys were.

When he'd done his rounds, Casey headed on up to the main house. He parked his truck and stood outside for a moment, the cool morning air soothing his mood. The sun hadn't risen very high in the sky, but the warm rays felt good on his shoulders. The curtain flicked, and he saw Ember standing by the kitchen window. She wore a gray sweater, her hair tumbling down around her shoulders, and those direct blue eyes followed him with a mildly curious expression.

"I can't put it off, Lord," he prayed under his breath. "Guide me."

Sometimes God expected His children to hand deliver a blessing to someone else. If only that particular blessing wasn't the one he'd been praying for, himself.

Casey headed to the side door and knocked once before opening it. Mr. Vern was seated at the table with his ledgers open as he worked through the ranch's monthly finances, and he glanced up as Casey came inside.

"Good morning," Mr. Vern said. "How's the herd?"

"Twelve new calves last night," Casey said. "All healthy."

"Good, good." Mr. Vern nodded, turning his attention back down to the ledger. "I'm just trying to get these accounts sorted out. I need to write a check for the nursing home."

"No problem, sir. I'm here to see if Ember's well enough to ride," Casey said, turning toward Ember. She stood by the counter, her bandaged foot gingerly touching the floor, but obviously not holding her weight. She took a sip from a mug.

"That depends on how much will be expected from me," she said.

"I'll get you in and out of the saddle," Casey said, and he had to admit, he was looking forward to any excuse to be close to her again.

"If that's the case, let's go." She put her mug down on the counter and turned to Mr. Vern.

"Thank you for breakfast, Mr. Vern."

The older man looked up with a distracted smile. "Not a problem." He pursed his lips. "Are you any closer to a decision on this place?"

"It's beautiful land, sir," Ember said. "But unless I can find some solid proof that the Harpers homesteaded here, I'm not going to put in an offer."

Mr. Vern nodded slowly. "All right, then. Thanks for being honest."

And he sank back down into his ledgers again. Casey looked at his boss for a moment, his heart going out to him. The financial pressure was heavy this time of year, and with his wife's medical care getting more expensive, Casey could only imagine the weight of those worries. But it would be over soon enough, and Mr. Vern would have his sale.

Casey helped Ember limp down the steps and into the waiting truck. He turned the key and the engine rumbled to life. Then he looked over at her. God worked things together for good—not just for a collective good, but for an individual's good, too. For a man with a heart that kept loving when it shouldn't, for two tiny boys whose parents were dead and for this woman who'd been through too much in her lifetime. God worked things together for good—Casey had to hold on to that.

Casey pulled out of the drive and headed down the

gravel road toward the red horse barn. He felt better with Ember by his side, even knowing that he was about to give her the keys to this place, figuratively speaking. What was it about Ember Reed that did this to him?

"How is your ankle on the bumps?" he asked. "Because on a horse, it'll be even worse."

"It's not too bad," she said. "It wasn't as bad of a sprain as I thought—or maybe it was the ice compress Mr. Vern gave me last night that fixed it right up. I expected to see all sorts of black-and-blue on my foot, but it's only a little bruised."

Casey was thankful to God for the small blessings—it could have been a whole lot worse. They fell into silence for a few more minutes as he circled around toward the barn. When they arrived, he pulled to a stop and leaned forward to look at the corral.

"I think this will be worth it for you," he said.

"Casey, I'm not a country woman," Ember said with a low laugh. "It might be easier to just tell me about whatever it is you think I need to see... Besides, I'm not sure I'm going to pursue this sale. I was praying about this pretty seriously out there by the river, and in response, I was attacked by wolves and sprained my ankle."

"Maybe that wasn't a response to your prayer," Casey replied.

"And maybe it was. I don't need to be shown any more rugged territory to convince me that I'm in over my head, Casey. You've already accomplished that."

"This isn't about proving that you don't belong here," he said with a shake of his head. "This is...just for you."

Casey got out of the vehicle and circled around to

help her down from the passenger side of the truck. She was warm in his arms as he helped her down, and he went ahead to open the door for her into the barn.

Casey had the horses saddled and ready, so all he had to do was help Ember up into the saddle. Once she was settled he looked up at her, drinking in this beautiful woman with the aching heart. She was lovely, interesting, tender, smart—the whole package. But she wasn't for him. He could be a part of answering her prayers, though, and today he'd get to see the look on her face when she saw the foundation of her family's homestead.

Those weren't his walls—they were hers.

He just prayed that while God was working out Ember's good, that He would remember Casey, too. Because he'd marched so long that every single part of him was deeply tired. Especially his heart.

Ember's ankle was a little sore as Patience started to move, following Casey's large stallion, but she wouldn't complain. She could tell that Casey wanted to show her something important, and the curiosity if she waited longer would be more agonizing than the ride, in her opinion. There was a throbbing place in her heart that wished she could find some proof that this had been the Harpers' land, but maybe Casey had found a hint that would mean something to her... Because it wasn't just about her therapy center—it was about coming home.

The day was bright and warm, and she could feel summer coming in that fragrant wind. She sucked in a chestful of spring air as Casey led them out of the corral and then through the gate.

"Are we going through the woods again?" Ember asked.

"No, we're heading across a pasture. It's through open fields," he replied. "It was when I was dealing with that difficult calving that I saw something you'll be interested in."

"And that's all you'll say?" she asked with a rueful smile.

"Yup." He grinned back at her.

"Are you sure this ranch won't kill me yet?" she asked with a low laugh.

"Not entirely," he replied, then chuckled. "I told you that ranch life wasn't what you were expecting. There is no living peaceably with nature. You live peaceably in spite of it, and you'd better know what you're doing."

"For every story in that old journal about catching crayfish in the creek and running around outside or befriending some animal, there was another story about someone just about dying," Ember said, her mind going back over those well-worn stories told and retold by her mother.

"Oh, yeah? Like who?" Casey said.

"Oh, like Bernard—that was the oldest son in the family. He went hunting with his father, and they shot an elk. He went up to finish it off and he got a hoof to the head. They had to carry him back to the house and bandage him up. He was unconscious for a week. They sent for a doctor from town who said he'd die. But he didn't. He eventually woke up. He was never the same, though. Walked with a limp, even though his leg hadn't been hurt, and he slurred his words. A brain injury, I'd imagine. They didn't have an explanation for it back then."

Ember sighed. Was she crazy to want this rugged, unforgiving patch of land? But even with the risks involved, if this was Harper land, then she did! She wanted to come home to those stories and the ancestors who battled the elements to make a life in these wild Montana plains.

"So why did your ancestors choose to come out here to homestead?" Casey asked.

"No idea," she admitted. "That was never mentioned. They just did. But I think it must have been a sense of adventure. Pa—that's what the journal called the father of the family—was the adventurous sort. He was the kind of man who could build a log cabin by himself with an ox and a hatchet. He was a big man—stood head and shoulders taller than anyone else—and he hardly ever talked. Mam adored him and did all the chatter for him. And she…trusted him to keep them all alive, I suppose."

The horses plodded comfortably forward, and Ember adjusted herself in the saddle, trying to find a better position for her ankle. She bent down to rub a hand over the tensor bandage. She was trusting Casey to keep her alive, too, so she felt like she could understand Mam a little better now. With the right man to rely on, a woman could face more than she ever thought possible.

"You sore?" Casey asked.

"Yeah." She winced. "I'll be okay."

"You want to stop and rest?" he asked, and there was concern in his voice. "I knew it was too early to take you on horseback."

"No, I'm fine," she said, forcing a smile. "I want to see—whatever it is you've got to show me. My car will be ready soon, and I have a feeling I've come close to outstaying my welcome with Mr. Vern, so if you have something to show me, I guess I'd better see it now."

Casey nodded, but the smile slipped from his face. "Yeah, of course."

"I doubt you want me around here getting in your way any longer than necessary, either," she said, trying to sound more jovial than she felt.

"I don't know about that," Casey said. "I've been getting used to you around here."

She smiled sadly at that. She'd been getting used to him, too. Maybe even more than that... It was hard not to lean into him, trust him. It was hard not to get comfortable in those arms.

Was that what she was looking for in her family land—a man of her own to stand by her side and fend off the wolves? If she was, she needed to stop that fantasy right now and see this ranch for what it was.

"I have patients who are waiting for me in Billings," she said. "I have a whole life waiting for me."

"I know," he said.

What was he thinking? She wished she knew, but his expression was granite and he rode facing straight ahead, his hat low and shielding his face from both the sun and her scrutiny.

"So tell me some family story of yours," she said.

"Is it going to say something about me?" he asked, shooting her a rueful smile.

"Very likely," she retorted. "But I told you mine, so you tell me yours."

Casey was silent for a moment, then said, "Okay... So when my grandfather was a teenager, he was in love with a girl from a rich ranching family. His dad wasn't rich—he worked his land with nothing to spare.

Anyway, so Grandpa decided to try to see the girl by sneaking onto her property and throwing rocks at her window to get her attention. He threw a rock too hard and it broke the windowpane. Her father let the dogs out, and they chased him all the way home."

"Did he marry her?" Ember asked with a smile.

"He went back the next day to pay for the window and apologize to her father in person. Her father yelled at him a bit, and the girl just stood there and watched. Grandpa said that's when he knew he could never marry her—a woman who just stood there and let someone else come down on him like that. Either she didn't have the gumption to stand up to her father—or she didn't love Grandpa enough to fight for him. Whichever it was, she wasn't the one for him."

"Who did he marry?"

"The girl at the ranch next door. They'd been friends for years, and she might not have been fancy, Grandpa said, but she once shot a wolf that was attacking his dog. He said a woman with an eye like that and steady trigger finger—he wanted her on his side in life."

Ember laughed softly. "I like that one."

"So what does it say about me?" Casey looked over at her, flicking his hat up higher on his forehead as he met her gaze.

"It says your family values ability over a pretty face," Ember said. And if that were the case, then whatever he felt for her would evaporate soon enough, because Ember didn't have that steady trigger finger. Maybe that was for the best.

Casey didn't answer, and they rode on in silence for a few more minutes, the horses plodding along at their own pace. Ember let her mind wander and she looked around at the mountains in the distance, the gently undulating hills and the crystal-clear sky that stretched over them.

There was a scattering of cows grazing and chewing their cud, and Ember smiled as she saw a calf drinking milk from its mother. The cow's eyes followed her as she rode past—that look both protective and doe-eyed all at once.

"Milk River is just over there—you can see the trees that line the bank."

"I see it." There was a faint sparkle of water that she could just make out through the foliage.

"This is where we'll dismount," Casey said, reining in his horse and swinging down from the saddle in one continuous movement. He made it look easy, and she looked down at the ground, which suddenly looked very far below her, and licked her lips nervously.

"I'll help you," Casey said. He held up a hand. "Take your sprained foot out of the stirrup and stand up on your good leg. You're going to swing it over just like you're coming down on your own."

"No, that's going to hurt—"

"Trust me," he interrupted her. "I'm not some kind of monster. Your foot will never hit the ground. I've got you."

Ember did as he'd instructed and put all of her weight on her good foot in the stirrup, then eased her injured foot out of the other stirrup and swung it around. The momentum kept her moving, and her stomach lurched as she started down to the ground. Before she'd gotten far, though, she felt Casey's strong arm scoop underneath her, and she landed solidly in his arms. She let out pent-up breath and looked up to find those dark eyes pinned to hers. Casey smiled slightly, then lowered her to the ground.

"There," he said.

"Thank you…" It hardly seemed like words enough to encompass how she felt about all the little things this big cowboy had been doing for her over the last week.

"Can you walk a bit?" he asked.

"Yes, I can hobble around," she said with a low laugh. "It's not graceful, but it's a lot better than it was."

Casey scooped her hand up in his warm palm. "Lean on me if it's easier," he said. "What I want to show you is just over here."

A young cow let out a moo and sauntered away from them as they made their way over lush grass. Casey tucked her hand into the crook of his arm, and he slowed his pace for her as she limped along. She could hear the sound of running water, even though she couldn't see the river from this vantage point. A cool breeze lifted her hair away from her face, and she looked around, wondering what he could possibly want to show her out here.

"Is it the herd?" she asked, looking up at him quizzically. "I don't get it—"

"Come on," he said with a shake of his head. "I wouldn't drag you all the way out here to see cattle. Give me more credit than that."

"Maybe you just wanted to get me alone for a bit," she said with a teasing smile.

Casey arched an eyebrow, then shrugged noncommittally. "I *did* want to get you alone. But it's more than that. Over here."

Casey led the way to a rocky area that looked scuffed, like it had been dug up a little recently. And when her gaze fell on those patterns of the exposed rock, she stopped short. It was a perfect rectangle—about the size of a packing box.

"What is it?" she asked breathlessly, looking up at Casey, and her heart sped up in her chest. She had a feeling she knew what it was, but she wanted him to say it.

"A fireplace hearth," he said. He pulled a trowel from his jacket pocket, sank down to his haunches and started to dig around the outside.

"A home—there was a house right here—" Ember looked around before her gaze came back to Casey, who dug steadily around the rocks, exposing mortar and more rock as he dug. "Casey—did you know about this before?"

"I had no idea," he said. "Even Mr. Vern didn't know about it. There aren't any stories about houses by the river…not that Mr. Vern ever mentioned. But there's more."

His trowel scraped raspily over rock, and then he tapped something that made a slightly different sound, and she bent down to get a better look. It was a single red brick. Her breath caught in her chest, and she stared at Casey, the words still formulating in her mind.

Ember let out a low laugh and shook her head. "This is it. You've found it—the homestead. The brick! Who else would have done that? The house was by the river, they said—walking distance to fetch fresh water. And behind them were the open plains where the wolves roamed at night and the buffalo would wander past in massive herds… This is it!"

Casey rose to his feet, the trowel still in his hand,

and she moved toward him, looking up into his eyes uncertainly.

"This is your proof," he said quietly.

"And you showed it to me—" Ember shook her head slowly. "You showed it to me, knowing what it meant—for you."

Casey's dark gaze met hers, and he reached up, touched her cheek with the pad of his thumb. "I told you that you could trust me."

Ember put her arms around his neck. She'd meant to simply go up on her tiptoes to hug him, but with her injured ankle, tiptoes weren't a possibility, so he came down to her, instead, and she found his face so close to hers, and she did the one thing she knew she shouldn't—she closed her eyes and touched her lips to his.

Casey gathered her up in his arms and kissed her back, the lowing of the cattle surfing the warm prairie wind that circled around them. This was Harper land, and she could feel it in her heart. But Casey showing her... That had been a bigger gesture than she could even comprehend right now. Her heart soared with excitement, and when Casey released her, she felt heat rush to her cheeks.

"I'm sorry," she said, hobbling back. "I shouldn't have—"

"Hey." Casey caught her hand in his, stopping her retreat. "It's okay. That was honest."

And it was. She met his eyes once more and found that warm gaze enveloping her.

"I have my proof," she said. "This is it—the land where all those stories took place. It's like my very own holy land."

"It's yours," he said quietly.

"Pa and Mam must have chosen this place, and I

can see why. They had no idea how many children they'd have, or how they'd make it each winter, but they managed." She looked around once more at the swell of the field and the jagged peaks beyond. Despite today's modern world, it was still so rugged, so vast. Even knowing this land was settled, she felt like a speck on the landscape.

"But what about you, Casey?" she asked quietly.

"I don't know what to say," he said, his eyes filled with sadness. "Fair is fair."

Chapter Thirteen

Ember went with Casey to church Wednesday evening for the farewell service. They sat in the back of the little country chapel, the babies sleeping in their arms as they had the week before.

"Would you like me to take the baby for a bit?" an older woman asked Ember with a smile.

Ember hesitated, then looked down into the dozy face of the tiny boy. He opened his mouth in a yawn, and she smiled down at him.

"Actually, I'd rather hold him," she said. "But thanks."

The woman moved off and Ember allowed herself the brief luxury of leaning into Casey's strong shoulder and enjoying Wyatt's sleepy warmth in her arms. She'd come to care for these babies more than any of them knew. They'd sunk into her heart, no matter how hard she tried to protect herself, and when she went back to the city again she'd miss them deeply.

Ember looked up at the stained-glass windows, her gaze following the pictures backlit by early evening sunlight. The first pane showed the Virgin Mary sitting with her son on her lap, and she sparkled with bright colors and obvious joy. The next pane showed her bowed by the foot of the cross, her heart breaking in a way only a mother could understand. And the last pane showed Mary in her iconic blue robe standing before the empty tomb, and those bright, glittering colors of wonder and happiness were back.

Mary was the mother every Christian woman looked to…the mother who had endured the deepest of all heartbreak, all for the sake of her son. Ember tore her eyes from the stained-glass windows. Sometimes, motherhood meant enduring untold pain like Mary had. Mary might not have said goodbye to her boy in infancy, but she'd had to relinquish him eventually, and it would have torn her heart in two.

Casey's little finger touched the side of Ember's hand, pulling her attention back to him. The movement was gentle, purposeful. She looked over at him, her heart swelling with sadness. His face was clean-shaven for church, and he smelled of the musky aftershave he must have used. His shirt was crisp and open at the neck, revealing his tanned skin. He caught her eye, and he slipped his hand over hers, warming hers. She wished she could freeze time, and she could avoid all the changes that were coming.

She'd miss Casey and the babies, and she realized that she'd worry about them a little bit, too. Would Casey's aunt understand Wyatt's need for snuggles after his bottle, or Will's curiosity and the way he liked to look around the room? When the infants cried for their mother, as Ember was convinced they still did, would Casey's aunt know why those little hearts were breaking?

But these babies weren't Ember's business—not officially. Casey would raise them, and he'd find appropriate childcare for them. He would find a job somewhere, and another ranch would benefit from his expertise... And she'd begin the process of setting up her own therapy center here on her family's land. Life would go on, and Ember's hopes and goals would be achieved.

So why wasn't she feeling happier about that? It was hard to feel the full impact of that joy because she'd be both putting a good number of men out of work, and moving forward in her goals without Casey Courtright in her life, and until a week ago, that would have meant nothing to her.

He shouldn't matter! But he did. He'd proved himself to be invaluable—he'd saved her life! He'd shown her the very spot where her family had built their homestead... He'd been her answer to prayer. He'd caught her when she was injured, carried her when she was weak and kissed her so tenderly that she'd melted under his touch. And yet he couldn't be her answer to *every* prayer.

Sure, just tell her heart that—it hadn't caught up.

This was a goodbye service for the current pastor—his last sermon to be preached in this church. Another pastor would come and lead this country parish, and the sentiment of goodbyes seemed appropriate this week.

The pastor's sermon wound up, and he sat down. The pianist went to her place at the old piano and began the prelude to the last hymn. The service was over.

"You okay?" Casey whispered as he picked up the worn hymnal and flipped it open.

Ember nodded. "I'll have to be."

"Do you want to head out early?" He leaned down to keep his words private.

Ember's heart was too full to stand there listening to those sweet old hymns and still be able to keep her emotions under control. She glanced around—the other parishioners had risen to their feet and the first swell of singing began.

"Let's go," she agreed softly, and Casey dropped her hand. Casey waited for Ember in the aisle, and then they slipped out the back door, leaving the service behind them as they headed for the freedom of sunshine.

Ember's ankle was still sore, but much better than before. They paused in the rosy wash of lowering sun and Casey got the car seats out of the truck.

"It might be easier if we can put them down," he said.

They got the babies settled into their seats, and then Casey nodded toward the fence line that cut off church property from a neighboring field.

"Let's go over there," he said.

Ember nodded. The babies were still fast asleep, and they ambled across the grass together. Casey put the car seats down on the grass by the fence, angling them so that the boys' faces stayed shaded. Across the grass, the piano could still be heard, the chords seeping out of the church and into nature. Toward the west, pink and red washed over the sky, the sun large on the horizon.

"You haven't put your offer in on the ranch yet," Casey said, breaking the quiet.

"Not yet," she admitted.

"Are you going to?" he asked.

Ember nodded. "Yes, I am. I just couldn't bring myself to do it yesterday. I don't know why…"

"It'll change this," he said, his voice low and hollow. "Us. It'll end whatever we're doing here."

"And what are we doing?" she asked, turning toward him. "We've crossed all professional lines, you know."

Casey looked down at her, then shrugged helplessly. "I don't know about you, but I've been falling for you something fierce."

Tears misted Ember's eyes and she shook her head. "We can't do this—"

"I think it's already done."

Ember put her hand on the rough wooden fence, and he slid a warm palm on top of hers. He was so confident, so comforting, and she tipped her head over onto his shoulder and heaved a sigh.

"Why won't you work for me, Casey?" she pleaded softly.

"I can't do it." His voice was low and filled with pain.

"And why not?" She lifted her head and looked up at him. "Are you just that stubborn?"

"I have a couple of good reasons," he said, still not looking at her. He was staring out into the rippling field of young, green wheat. "The first is that I'm a rancher, not some city-slicker babysitter."

"That's harsh, but fine," she said. "And the second reason?"

"I fell in love with you." He finally looked over at her, those dark eyes drilling into hers, and he sighed. "Against all my better judgment, might I add."

"You…" she breathed. "You love me?"

"I didn't say it was logical or right," he replied with a shake of his head. "But yes."

And it suddenly all fell into place for her. She could

see it come together, and this missing piece explained it all—her misery, her inability to embrace the blessings she had because they didn't include the tall, protective cowboy in the picture.

"I love you, too," she said, the words catching in her throat, and Casey turned and pulled her into his arms, his lips covering hers with a kiss of longing and anguish. He kissed her long and slow, and when he pulled back, she saw tears glistening in his eyes.

"Isn't there some way we could make this work?" he pleaded. "Some loophole here that will let us live happily together in spite of it all?"

She wished that there were... If she had a couple in therapy facing the challenges they were facing, would she see a solution that they were missing out on? But no—not every relationship was salvageable. Not every couple who loved each other could make it last for a lifetime. There were heartbreaking times when love just wasn't enough.

Ember shook her head and put a hand in the center of his chest, pushing herself back out of his arms.

"No," she whispered. "There isn't."

Casey put a hand over her fingers in the center of his chest, but she tugged them free, and his heart ached as she stepped back. She licked her lips and looked down at her feet, then limped another step back. Ember Reed was so stubborn, yet so vulnerable. He longed to hold her again, but she didn't want his touch, and he let his hand fall to his side.

"What makes you so sure?" he demanded. He needed a reminder of all the reasons why they wouldn't work because right now, he couldn't remember a single good reason why he shouldn't gather her up in his arms and simply claim her as his.

"We want different things, Casey," she said, her chin trembling ever so little. "I want my therapy center, and that goes against everything you want in life! It goes against your vision for this county, everything you value and respect—"

"Then run a ranch with me," he said. "There's honor in feeding the nation, in raising cattle—"

"And there is honor in helping families to reconnect!" she interrupted him. "It's what I do, Casey. It's not going away!"

"I'm not saying there isn't honor in what you do," he said feebly.

"Also, you need a mother for those babies."

Those words landed more heavily than anything else, and he looked down at the sleeping boys in their car seats, their long lashes brushing chubby cheeks. Will was opening and closing one little fist as he slumbered, and Wyatt heaved one tiny, shuddering sigh. Those boys needed a mother... He needed a woman to parent with him. She was right there. But he'd been watching her blossom with the babies over the last couple of days, and he shook his head.

"Ember, you *could* love them..."

"I daresay I already do," she said, wiping a tear from her cheek. "But I can't do it, Casey. I can't be a mother to another child. Don't you understand what I did when I gave up my little boy? I shut the door on motherhood—"

"And maybe that was a mistake!" he countered.

"Mistake or not, it was a choice I made!" she shot back. "And don't say I was too young to make it, because at the age of twenty I could have joined the army or gotten married! I was plenty old enough to make a life-altering decision. I know you want to think the best of me, Casey, but I had nine months to think it through. And yes, I regret it—deeply. But that's the choice I made, and I can't just back out on it. I can't stand in as mother to your boys, because I wouldn't be a good one, Casey. They deserve better than what I can offer."

"You could be—" he began.

"No!" Tears shone in her eyes and she shook her head vehemently. "Because every single time I look at those babies, I think of my own! I can do it for a few days. I can put my heart aside for a little while, but for the rest of my life? I *am* a mother, Casey, but I'm not a good one."

"But you love me," he said, his voice almost a growl.

"I love you," she said with a teary nod. "But it isn't enough."

The church doors opened and the first few people came outside, chatting voices floating over the grass-scented breeze toward them. They weren't alone anymore, and Casey straightened, then shot Ember one more miserable look.

"So what now?" he asked softly.

"I'll submit my offer in the morning."

Casey nodded, a lump shutting off his throat.

"And if you changed your mind and agreed to work for me—"

"No, Ember." No matter how much he longed to change his mind right now, he knew he'd only regret it. He couldn't be her manager, her protector, her source of advice. He couldn't work for her, next to her, feeling as he did and knowing it was hopeless. It would be torture, and he'd get hardened and meaner…or he'd weaken in his own moral resolves. He didn't want to be that man.

"Then I'll go back to Mr. Vern's house and I'll pack up," she said with a quiver in her voice. "I got a text from the auto shop before the service started. My car is done. I'll pick it up in the morning, after I've talked to Mr. Vern. I can finish up the sale from Billings. I've seen what I needed to see, thanks to you, Casey."

"Will I see you before you go?" he asked softly.

"If you want to—" she met his gaze, then pressed her lips together as if trying to hold back tears "—if you don't think it would be hard for nothing…"

"It wouldn't be for nothing," he said curtly. "It would be for a proper goodbye."

"Okay."

More people were flooding out of the church now, and a few were looking over at them in curiosity. This was a small community, and gossip would fly around the rural community like wildfire. Casey sighed.

"Let me drive you back to the ranch, then," he said.

It would be a difficult drive, sitting next to the woman he loved but couldn't be with.

She'd buy the ranch, and Casey would have to build his life somewhere else. Just not next to her, because he couldn't endure any more heartbreak.

Chapter Fourteen

Ember hadn't slept much the night before. She'd lain awake listening to the sound of wind outside, the soft moan that echoed her own heartbreak. Falling for Casey had been a bad idea, but it hadn't been a choice. There was something about Casey that filled a part of her heart that she hadn't peeked into before. He'd opened his heart to her, too, and that made this all the harder. If a few vital things had been different, she'd have married him.

"Did I really just think that?" she murmured. Morning had dawned clear and unforgiving. She stood in front of a small mirror, checking her makeup. Some concealer under her eyes and some powder seemed to cover most of the evidence of last night's tears, but she still felt puffy.

Loving Casey wasn't going to just go away because they knew it wouldn't work. She realized that. And now, instead of grieving for her son, she was grieving for her son, the man she'd fallen in love with and the tiny babies who had stolen her heart. Vern Ranch would never be the same for her again, because every single inch of this place had Casey's fingerprints on it.

"But it's still mine," she reminded herself. "Or it will be…"

Feelings passed. They didn't last forever. Eventually, she would be able to put this all behind her. Harper women carried on, even when it hurt.

So Ember went out into the kitchen, where Mr. Vern had just returned from his morning inspection of his land, and she handed him her official offer. Mr. Vern took the papers from her hand, scanned them and then shook her hand with enthusiasm.

"I'm thrilled, I have to say!" Mr. Vern enthused. "I wasn't sure you'd find what you were looking for on this land."

"Casey was the one who found the ruins of my family's homestead," Ember said. "So we have him to thank."

"Really now?" Mr. Vern nodded slowly. "And what about hiring him on as your manager?"

"He's been very clear about that," she admitted. "I'd love to have him work for me, but he's not interested."

"Ah." The smile slipped from his lined face, and then he shook his head. "All the same, I'm very happy to be selling this ranch to you, Miss Reed. These acres have been good to me, and I wish you only the best in your future endeavors here." The older man tapped the sheaf of papers he held in his hands. "I suppose we'll leave it up to the lawyers now, but I anticipate this being smooth and uncomplicated."

"I'm sure it will be." She forced a smile. There were no issues financially, at least. "I got a text yesterday saying that my car is fixed. I was wondering if you'd be willing to give me a ride into town to pick it up? I'll stay at a hotel tonight, and I'll be back in the morning to sign any more papers the lawyers send us."

"You wouldn't rather Casey give you that ride?" Mr. Vern asked. "You two seemed to have a special friendship."

"No." She swallowed quickly and dropped her gaze. "He's busy, and I'd rather not bother him."

"Ah." Mr. Vern looked at her a little more closely. "He's a good man, you know. Honest, stable, reliable."

"I know." Ember looked up sadly. "He's a very good man. But still, sir, I'd rather just go get my car this morning, if it's all the same to you. But if you're busy, I'm sure I can get a taxi from Victory to come out here—"

"No, no!" Mr. Vern said with a shake of his head. "A taxi... Of course I will drive you myself. I only thought—which doesn't matter. Obviously, I thought wrong. Let's get going now. I'll drop you off on the way to see my lawyer."

Ember smiled. "That sounds perfect. I do appreciate your hospitality, Mr. Vern. You've been very kind to host me the last week and a half."

"It was my pleasure, ma'am," Mr. Vern said, and he gave her a nod, his eyes sparkling.

Mr. Vern drove Ember into Victory. It was a forty-minute drive, and when they reached the auto shop, Ember thanked Mr. Vern for the ride, then went into the mechanic's office to pay her bill and pick up her car. It would feel good to be self-sufficient again with her own vehicle, and as she paid with her credit card, the realization that she was about to own all four hundred and two acres of the Vern ranch was just settling into her mind.

It wouldn't be the Vern ranch anymore. It would be the Harper Family Therapy Center. She'd already decided on the name when her dream for the place took root—professional enough to make the purpose for her therapy center evident, but with the personal addition of her mother's last name, too. The Harper women were strong—they were survivors. And that was the spirit she hoped to instill in the guests at her new, rural practice. She might have her father's last name, but she'd been raised by a single mother. Her mother's spirit was what guided her in her ambitions and hopes, not the Reed money.

Ember was hungry, and she decided to stop and get some breakfast at a diner before she went to find a hotel.

The streets of Victory were narrow, and there only appeared to be two or three stoplights in the entire town. Main Street was lined by clapboard-fronted buildings, and the parking spots in front of stores were all filled with dusty pickup trucks. Her car felt tiny compared to all the other vehicles. Over that last week she'd started to enjoy riding around in a pickup, high above the road. She just might take Mr. Vern's advice and get a shiny new Ford—not that it would stay shiny for long on these roads.

Pop's Diner was on the corner, and Ember pulled into a parking spot between a pickup truck and a U-Haul truck. She got out of her car and headed into the diner.

There weren't many patrons this morning—a scattering of men in blue jeans and trucker hats, and a family over by the window. The mother was facing in

Ember's direction; the father and a boy were sitting with their backs to her. There was something about that family that drew her attention more than the others— the mother's face. She wasn't just gentle and laughing at something with a sparkle in her eyes... She was familiar. Ember *knew* her.

"You can just take a seat anywhere," the waitress said with a smile on her way past with a pot of coffee in each hand. "I'll take your order in a minute, hon."

"Sure. Thanks," Ember said distantly, and it was then that the woman lifted her gaze and saw Ember. She froze, the laughter slipping from her face. Ember watched the emotions clamber over the other woman's features—shock, fear, uncertainty. No, seeing Ember was not good news—not to Sue Mitchell.

Sue looked toward her husband, murmured something, and then both husband and son turned and looked at her. The boy—he was the one who had Ember's attention. He had a rumple of curly brown hair and big dark eyes. He looked at her with mild curiosity— obviously not knowing who she was—then turned back to his plate.

"Who's that, Mom?" Ember heard him say, his voice floating over the din of the restaurant.

Sue got up from their table and came across the dining room toward Ember. She glanced back at her family once, and her husband's gaze was locked on them, his expression filled with trepidation. What they thought, Ember had no idea. Did they think she'd followed them or something?

"Ember?" Sue said quietly when she reached her. "What are you doing here?"

"I could ask you the same thing," Ember said, dragging her gaze back to the woman in front of her. "I just put an offer down on a piece of land out here. What are you doing in Victory?"

"You're..." Sue swallowed. "You're moving out here, then?"

"Yes." Ember looked back toward the table. The boy was putting his attention into his food, and Ember's heart sped up, all of this hammering home into her brain. "Is that Steven?"

"Yes." Sue took Ember's arm and tugged her farther away from the table, closer to the door. "He doesn't know who you are, Ember. We didn't tell him your name. He knows he's adopted, but we said we'd tell him more when he got older."

"I'm not here to find you," Ember said, pulling her arm out of the other woman's grasp. "I had no idea you were even located out here."

Her gaze whipped back to the table. Even though she'd suspected from the moment she saw Sue, the confirmation still bowled her over. That was him? That was her boy?

"We're just moving into town," Sue said. "You might as well know that my husband is the new pastor for Victory Country Church. It's out in the country, about half an hour from town."

"You're the new pastoral family—" Ember breathed.

"Yes." Tears rose in Sue's eyes. "Ember, I know that when we adopted Steven, we agreed to no contact. I know you didn't want to see us—it would have been harder, you said. So I never got the chance to properly thank you for the gift you gave us in that little boy. He's our treasure. And he's such a sweet kid! He's smart and kind..."

Ember looked toward the table again. The pastor was dropping some bills onto the table, and Steven was standing up.

"Is he happy, though?" Ember asked suddenly, her throat tightening with emotion. "Is he…? Did he miss me very much? I've been worrying about how hard it must have been at first—I know, it was ten years ago, but in some ways it feels like yesterday still."

"He's very happy," Sue replied.

"But that first night—the first few weeks…" Ember could hear the pleading in her own voice. Didn't Sue understand the misery that Ember had carried with her after that day?

"I stayed up with him all night that first night," Sue said softly. "And Ted stayed up all night the next night. We just held him and talked to him and sang to him. We wanted him to feel awash in love. We knew it would be hard on him, too, so we did our best to make sure he knew that he was as loved as humanly possible in our home. I promise you that. The third night, he slept, and when he woke up we both got up with him because we just wanted to look at him…"

Tears welled in Ember's eyes. They'd loved him as hard as they could—that helped, somehow.

Sue looked back at her approaching husband and son. "I'm going to introduce you, but we haven't told him yet—"

"Yes, you already said," Ember acknowledged. "Don't worry. I don't want to upset him, either."

Sue nodded, and as Ted and Steven approached, Sue pasted a smile on her face.

"Ted, you remember Ember, don't you? Steven, this is an old friend of ours—Ember Reed."

Steven looked up at her, clear eyes meeting hers. "Hi," he said and held out a hand to shake hers.

Ember took his fingers in her own and tried to drink in every detail of his rounded, boyish face. He looked like her a little bit—in the eyes, she thought. He didn't have her blond hair, but he had her cheekbones and fair complexion.

"Hi, Steven," Ember said, swallowing back her own emotion. "I haven't seen you in—in a long time."

"I don't remember you," he said, frowning slightly and tugging his hand back.

"You wouldn't," Ember said. "You were pretty tiny. But it's great to meet you now—all grown-up."

"Almost grown-up," he corrected her, and Ember laughed softly.

"Almost." She glanced toward his parents—the couple who had raised and loved him in her absence. She had so much she wanted to say to her son, but now was not the time. Her emotions weren't his problem, and she wouldn't make them a burden for him. "What grade are you in?"

"Five," he said. "Almost in grade six."

"Do you like school?" she asked.

"I'm starting a new one." He grimaced. "I don't like that."

"Well, Steven and I are going to go get that truck started," Ted said, reaching out to shake Ember's hand. Then he stopped short and opened his arms in a hug. He pulled her in close, patted her back a few times, then released her. "Ember, thank you. It's good to see you again."

Steven looked up at his dad questioningly, and then

the pair walked out of the diner toward the U-Haul, father's arm around son's shoulder.

"So he's doing well?" Ember asked, her voice shaking slightly as she followed the back of her son's retreating form. *Her son.* That was him. She felt a wash of pride. He'd turned out well.

"He's doing great," Sue confirmed. "He's healthy and strong. He's always been popular at school, too, so I'm not worried about this new school at all. He's nervous, but he'll do great."

Ember nodded quickly, and she looked over at Sue, her eyes brimming with tears. "Thank you for being his mom," she whispered.

"Thank you for giving me the honor," Sue said, and she wrapped her arms around Ember. The women clung to each other for a moment. Then Sue released her and stepped back. "If you're going to be in the area, Ted and I had better have a talk with Steven about you."

"I won't get in the way," Ember said quickly.

"But he'll want to know you, too," Sue replied. "He's been asking more about you lately, and it just seems—the timing seems providential, is all."

"A little," Ember agreed with a misty smile.

"Here—" Sue dug into her purse and pulled out a card. "That's my cell phone number. Call me if you want to. I guess you know where to find us. But give us a few weeks to have some talks with Steven first, if you don't mind."

"That's fine." Ember nodded quickly. "Thanks. This is my card."

Ember pulled out her own and passed it over. Sue scanned it, her eyebrows rising. "Therapist?"

"I got that degree, and then some," Ember said.

"I'm happy for you, Ember." A smile radiated over Sue's face. "Really happy. You've done well for yourself. I hope all your dreams come true."

"I'm not sure I deserve them—" The words were out before Ember could think better of them, and she felt heat rush to her face. She was saying too much.

"Deserve them?" Sue shook her head slowly. "Ember, you gave us the most personal, painful gift that anyone could give. You made it possible for me to be a mom. You *chose* me—and for that I will owe you my life. Being Steven's mom—he's my world. That sacrifice doesn't make you weak, Ember. It makes you *strong*! You deserve happiness—the whole package. All of it! I don't want to overstep here, but I'm going to be praying that God gives you all of your heart's desires. Every last one!"

"Will he hate me?" Ember asked uneasily.

"Our Steven?" Sue shook her head. "He doesn't know your name, but he knows that while his birth mom wasn't in a place to be able to raise him, she loved him with her whole heart. So she made the hardest choice in the world and made our dreams come true instead of her own. He knows that his adoption was wrapped in love from the very start, and that his birth mom is our hero."

A tear slipped down Ember's cheek.

"Mom!" Steven's voice sounded faintly from outside, and Ember's heart leaped at the sound. Through the glass door, Ember could see Steven hanging out the window of the U-Haul.

Sue waved and smiled, then turned back to Ember. "I'd better go."

Ember wiped the tear from her cheek. "Yes—they're waiting."

"We'll be in touch, I'm sure," Sue said, and with one last little flutter of her fingers in a wave, she walked from the diner and outside into the sunlight. Ember watched as she hopped up in the U-Haul truck and gave her son a kiss on his cheek.

Her son was loved, cherished even. And he was okay.

In her heart, instead of a newborn's frantic wails, she thought she could hear a lullaby sung by a brand-new mom and dad who had never left her baby alone, not even for a minute. God had answered all of Ember's prayers for her tiny boy through the love of adoptive parents.

Sue had loved Steven, opened her heart to him and anticipated all his needs. Even now—she was willing to give Steven a chance to get to know his biological mom…and why? Because he would need it.

Back on the Vern ranch, there were two baby boys who needed love. And maybe, just maybe, their mother had sent up one last prayer of her own, much like Ember's. Was it possible to open her heart to those little boys and become the mom they needed so desperately? Could *she* be the answer to their mother's heart-deep prayer like Sue had been for hers?

Ember felt something inside of her lift, and a new yearning took root in her heart. She was a mother—she always would be—but a mother's heart grew with each child she loved. Maybe there was a chance that Ember could be a mother again.

She wasn't ready to pray for that new yearning. She'd only just recognized it deep under all that pain. But maybe one day God would fulfill that wish, too.

But it wouldn't be with Casey, much as she loved him. Even if she could accept his babies and be a mother to them, he couldn't accept her career or her dreams for the future. It wouldn't work. Not this time.

She'd just have to trust her heart to God.

Casey poured two mugs of coffee and nudged one in Bert's direction across the kitchen table. Outside, the sun had set, but there was still a smudge of crimson along the horizon. Casey's heart was heavy. Ember had left that morning, taking her bags with her, and she hadn't said goodbye.

"So Mr. Vern sold the place, did he?" Bert asked, taking a sip of coffee.

"He accepted Ember's offer this morning." Casey sighed.

"I'm sorry you lost out on your chance to own this ranch, Casey. I know how much it meant to you," Bert said.

"Yeah. Well." What else was there to say?

"And that Miss Reed," Bert went on. "There was something between you, wasn't there?"

"It wouldn't last," Casey said. "She has her own issues around motherhood and she can't be an adoptive mom to these boys. Obviously, that wouldn't work between us."

"Obviously," Bert agreed. "Was that all?"

Casey smiled bitterly. "Whatever I feel for her, it isn't enough, Bert. She and I want different things. I want to raise these boys on a ranch with cattle drives and morning chores. She wants to set up some therapy center..."

"What's wrong with a therapy center?" Bert asked. "It's something to help the families around here."

"Families need to work!" Casey shot back. "They need employment and self-respect. I'm not saying this center wouldn't be beneficial for the city folk who never get out into the open air, but for us? For the locals?"

Bert was silent. One of the babies started to whimper and Casey scraped his chair back and handed a prepared bottle to the old ranch hand. "Care to take a baby?"

"Sure."

Casey went over to Will, who had woken up, big eyes blinking and his little mouth opening and shutting as he searched for milk.

"Hey, buddy," Casey said softly, scooping him out of his cradle. "You hungry?"

Will let out a little frustrated cry, and Casey handed him to Bert, who expertly tucked the infant into the crook of his arm and popped a bottle into his mouth. Will slurped away immediately.

Then Casey went and picked up Wyatt. It was better to wake this sleeping baby and feed them both at the same time, or he'd be up every hour overnight feeding one baby at a time. Wyatt blinked his eyes open as Casey lifted him from his cradle and put him up onto his shoulder as he came back to the table.

"Fiona and I went to a therapist for the better part of a year," Bert said after a moment, his eyes still pinned on the baby in his arms, slurping away on the bottle.

"You—" Casey cleared his throat. "Seriously?"

"It was after our daughter was killed in that car accident. We just couldn't... It was too big of a loss, and we weren't talking to each other because we didn't want to make it worse, I guess, and it was just eating us up."

"I didn't realize that," Casey said quietly, and he adjusted Wyatt in his arms and offered the baby his bottle.

"Therapists just help you talk about stuff," Bert said. "I wasn't any good at that. And if I hadn't learned how, I wouldn't have stayed married real long. So you could say that therapist saved our marriage."

Casey eyed the big cowboy, who still refused to look up. "Cowboys don't talk much, Bert. We ride."

"Well, maybe we should talk more," the older man replied. "Maybe *you* should talk more."

"Me?" Casey asked in surprise.

"What are you wanting to give those boys on a ranch?"

"A country upbringing," he retorted. "You know what I'm talking about."

"Yeah, well, spell it out for me," Bert replied.

"I want them to learn perseverance, fortitude, morals, how to stick with something even when the weather's against them," Casey said. "All the stuff you learn when you're raised on a ranch with chores and 4-H. It's a priceless childhood."

"And what about communication?" Bert asked. "Because that's mighty important once these tykes grow up and get married. What about flexibility? What about softness?"

"I'll throw that in, too, I guess. Or I'll try," Casey replied with a rueful smile. "What are you getting at, Bert? I'm not married yet. I don't have a woman to bring in the feminine stuff for me."

"You're so focused on the upbringing you had,

Casey, that you're forgetting you had a mother who raised you with lessons of her own outside what you got from your father. Perseverance is important, but so is flexibility. I grew up watching my dad stay the course, and I never stopped to think that the course could change if you needed it to. Bending isn't weakness, Casey. It's making room for another person in your life."

"And you think—" Casey started.

"I think you love her," Bert finished for him. "And don't even bother arguing that, because I know it's true."

"I'm not arguing," Casey said with a sigh. "But, Bert, ranching is in my blood!"

"And that woman is in your heart," Bert replied. "You want to raise those boys alone and teach them to be rock-hard cowboys? You can do it. Or you can raise them with a woman you love—a woman worth bending for—and you can teach them how to be successful in more than just their work. Because a home life matters, too. No cowboy is fully content coming back to an empty house. Those boys need to learn how to fill their hearts as well as their barns."

Casey looked down at Wyatt's face as he drank the last of the bottle. He put the bottle on the table, then tipped Wyatt up onto his shoulder to burp him. His mind was spinning.

"You know how long I've wanted to own my own ranch, Bert?" Casey asked, his voice tight.

"Yup," Bert replied. "But life is long, and you've got a lot more years ahead of you than you do behind you. There will be other ranches, and who knows what the future holds? But will there be another woman who makes you feel like she does?"

"The pastor preached about Jericho's walls," Casey said. "They marched and they marched until they must have felt like they were going crazy. I've been marching, too—circling my own Jericho walls. After all that marching—to just give up—"

"There's faith in God to answer our prayers," Bert said, "and then there's faith in God when He gives us the unexpected. Maybe you prayed for land, but God saw fit to give you a lifelong love instead."

A lifelong love… It may very well be! Casey didn't see any easy way to stop loving her, but she didn't want what he could offer—and she didn't want to be a part of this little family. It was very likely a lifelong love, and he'd be measuring women against her for the rest of his life, but it didn't change those basic facts.

"It's not going to work out, Bert," Casey said gruffly.

Bert nodded. "Okay. Sorry to pry. I'll keep my peace."

But it got Casey to thinking…maybe there was more than one way to raise a kid right, and more than one way to find a heart-deep satisfaction in life. It had always been about the land before, but what if he had to choose between the dirt beneath his boots and the woman in his arms?

What if he'd been circling his Jericho walls and God had wanted to show him another way? What if God had other plans for his life that didn't include a ranch to run? Would he have faith enough to follow?

Chapter Fifteen

Ember printed off the documents her lawyer sent her on the printer in the hotel office. She thanked the manager and left him a tip for his trouble. She spent the next hour reading over the contract, making sure she understood exactly what she was signing with her lawyer on the phone explaining the details. And when she was ready, she got in her car and followed her GPS to Vern Acres.

As she drove up to the main house, her heart was in her throat, and not because she was buying this ranch, either. Somehow, that personal achievement had paled in comparison to her feelings for Casey. She'd promised that she'd say goodbye, but this parting would be a difficult one.

Would he even be here? She'd called ahead and told Mr. Vern that she was coming. He'd asked if he could tell Casey, and she'd agreed. Would he want to see her? Or would he rather avoid her altogether? She wasn't sure she'd blame him if he didn't come...

Ember parked her car and got out. The warm air ruffled through her hair, and she looked around, soaking up the view. The trees, the looming jagged mountain peaks… One day soon this view would just be home. She started toward the house and the side door opened. It wasn't Mr. Vern who came out, but Casey.

He'd come! Her breath caught in her throat as he stepped outside and headed toward her. That dark gaze locked on to hers, and he closed the distance between them and wrapped his arms around her, not saying a word. His lips came down over hers, so warm and strong and confident. She closed her eyes and sank into his embrace…but this wouldn't make their goodbye any easier. She reluctantly pulled back.

"No…" she said, her eyes brimming with tears. "Don't toy with me, Casey. We've been through this—"

"I know." He stepped back, his eyes still locked on hers pleadingly. "I'm sorry. I just— I'll stop doing that when I see you in town or whatever. I promise."

It was true—she'd see him around. Even if he didn't work for her, maybe he'd work in the area. Ember looked down at the pages in her hands.

"The final papers?" Casey asked.

"Yeah…" She sucked in a breath. "Casey, I saw my son."

He blinked at her, then squinted. "What?"

"The new pastor of the church and his wife—the Mitchells. That's the couple who adopted my son ten years ago. And I saw them in Pop's Diner."

"You're kidding!" Casey shook his head. "That must have been… Are you okay after that? Are you— I mean—" He didn't seem to know how to put it all into words, but she could feel the depth of his concern.

"I'm okay," she said. "It was so wonderful to see him. He's tall for his age, I think. He's got this headful of curly brown hair—it's so cute. And the big brown eyes. He's beautiful. And he's happy. That was my biggest worry, that he'd be empty and searching because of what I did, but he's not. He's a happy kid. He's definitely loved."

"That's awesome," Casey said, and he reached a hand out and ran a finger down her cheek. "I'm glad you got that."

"It changed things—" Ember wasn't sure if it was even fair to bring this up. They'd already gone over why they'd never work as a couple, but she was still so overflowing from the experience that she felt she had to talk to someone, and there was no one but Casey who she wanted to share this with.

"Changed what?" he murmured, stepping closer.

"I prayed every day for my son," she said softly. "I prayed so hard, and I loved him just as hard... I wanted to make up for not being there. But when I saw Sue and Ted again, and when she told me how they'd stayed up with him around the clock to make sure he didn't feel alone in those first few days... Casey, *they* were the answer to my prayers!"

"That's beautiful," he said quietly. "I like that."

"And I know it doesn't change anything else, Casey, but it does change whether or not I could be a mom again. I didn't want to betray my son on some level, but I realized that he has a mom now—and it's Sue."

"Wait—" Casey's voice lowered, and he put his hands on her shoulders. "Are you saying you've changed your mind about that?"

"Wyatt and Will *had* a mom," Ember tried to explain. "If she were able, I'm sure her very last prayer would have been for her boys, too. Sue was the answer to *my* prayers, and if all things were equal, I think I'd like to be the answer to that mom's prayers." She blinked back tears. "But I know it doesn't change the rest. I know that. I shouldn't even have brought it up."

Casey stepped closer again and ran a tendril of her hair through his fingers. "I've had a good talk with Bert, too."

"His job—" she started.

"No, not about his job. He's happy to retire, apparently. This was about me. He had a whole lot to say, and it all made sense. Thing is, I've been so focused on owning my own land for so long that I counted my own faith in God's ability to give me my desires as if God had promised me that land. But what if God wants something different for me? What if—" Casey smiled hesitantly. "What if God had brought me the woman He'd created for me instead of giving me a ranch?"

Ember's heart sped up in her chest, and she stared at Casey, dumbstruck.

"Thing is," Casey went on, "I've wanted to teach the boys the perseverance and steadfastness you learn on a ranch—very important character traits, might I add. But Bert pointed out that flexibility will give them happy marriages." He smiled regretfully. "And that's important, too."

"What are you saying, exactly?" Ember asked, shaking her head. "Because you're going to have to spell this out for me—"

"I'm saying I love you," Casey said, his voice cracking with emotion. "I'm saying that if you could love Wyatt and Will and raise them with me, then I can be flexible on the ranching issue. I can help you run your therapy center, and keep your clients alive long enough to sort out their family issues."

Ember's eyes welled with tears. "You'd do that?"

"Like Bert says—there will be other ranches. But a woman like you? That's once in a lifetime, Ember."

Casey stepped closer again, this time closing the distance between them as he wrapped his arms around her once more. "I love you."

"I love you, too," she whispered.

"Then marry me..."

Ember stared at him, then twined her arms around his neck and pulled that tall cowboy down to her level, where she kissed him with all the love pent up in her heart. He wrapped his arms around her waist and stood up straight, plucking her straight off the ground. Ember laughed, looking into those dark, tender eyes.

"Maybe there's a way to combine a working ranch with a therapy center," Ember said as her feet touched the ground again. "I'm not sure about the details, but if we put our heads together—"

"First things first," he said, a smile turning up the corners of his lips. "Say you'll marry me, Ember. Mrs. Ember Courtright. I think that sounds good."

"I think it sounds wonderful!" she said, tears glistening in her eyes. "Yes. I'll marry you, Casey."

Casey's lips covered hers once more as the screen door slammed behind them. They turned to see Mr. Vern standing on the step, a broad smile on his face.

"Is there news?" he asked with a grin.

"Let's go buy a ranch," Ember whispered, and Casey grinned.

"That sounds good to me. But keep it in your name.

I don't want you ever thinking I married you for your land."

Together they walked toward the house, and Ember's heart finally felt full to overflowing. She'd sign the papers that would set Mr. Vern free to pursue his retirement with his ailing wife, and then Ember knew exactly what she wanted to do...

She was going to pick up those baby boys and snuggle them close, and she'd be the mother they needed so badly. Sometimes God gave second chances, and as He twined hearts together, He answered prayer after prayer with the love that joined them.

Ember and Casey went inside. She looked around that ranch house, at the floors that had seen so many cowboy boots, at the kitchen that had fed so many, and she knew that she was home. But the fixture that made this house the home she wanted to settle into was the tall cowboy who stood by the kitchen table as Mr. Vern signed the last of the papers finalizing the sale. Casey Courtright was the one who filled her heart.

She loved him—with everything in her being. And somehow, in one visit to a Montana ranch, God had given Ember more than a goal realized; He'd given her a family.

Epilogue

On a warm, sunny day in mid-September when the heat from summer had dissipated, but the warmth still clung to the earth in defiance of the coming winter, Ember and Casey got married in the Victory Country Church.

The sermon was short, but it was on a topic very close to Casey's heart—Joshua marching around the walls of Jericho. This pastor took the story a little bit further, pointing out that Rahab, the Jericho woman who helped the spies and escaped destruction, ended up married— possibly to one of the spies themselves. That was what the Biblical records pointed to in Matthew, at least—a little bit of romance in the midst of that battle story. The walls came down, and between the lines there seemed to be a wedding. A little bit like Casey and Ember's story. Sometimes walls crumbled and hearts healed at the same time.

Almost everyone was in attendance for the Courtright-Reed wedding, and the pews were packed. Ember's father didn't make it, but he did send a very generous monetary gift. Casey's father was there, as was half the population of the town. Pastor Ted Mitchell took Ember and Casey through the most important vows of their lives.

"Do you take this woman to be your lawfully wedded wife, to have and to hold, in sickness and in health, for better or for worse, for richer or for poorer, as long as you both shall live?"

"Sure do," Casey said softly, fixing Ember with a tender smile.

"And do you, Ember, take this man to be your husband…"

Ember nodded, tears misting her eyes. "I do."

"Then I now pronounce you husband and wife. Feel free to kiss your bride, Casey."

Casey didn't seem to need any encouragement there, because he stepped forward and slipped his arms around her waist, pulling her close in a kiss, as clapping and cheers rose up from the guests in attendance.

Ember smiled up into her husband's eyes, and then they faced the church of friends and family.

"I'm pleased to be the first to introduce Mr. and Mrs. Casey and Ember Courtright!" Pastor Mitchell said. Casey squeezed her hand, and they headed down the aisle together. Ember had never felt quite so happy.

After the service was over, their photographer took them to a few different spots to take photos—by the church doors, standing with family, over by the rippling waves of golden wheat at the fence…

The babies were being held by various women in the family who passed them around and snuggled them close, but by the time they made it to the field for photos, Will and Wyatt had started to fuss, and Ember's heart followed them with every lusty cry.

They were bigger babies now—already seven months

old and full of personality—and Ember looked up at Casey.

"Time for some Courtright family photos?" she suggested softly.

"That sounds about right," Casey agreed, and they went to fetch their boys. Will and Wyatt stopped crying as soon as they were back in their parents' arms. And as the flash went off, recording this moment when her heart was so very full, Ember looked out at a group of kids who were observing the photos being taken, and she spotted Steven. He stood a little to the side, watching them wistfully. His parents had told him who she was, and they'd talked a few times about why she'd made that difficult choice…

"Maybe we could get a picture with the minister's family, too," Ember said to the photographer. "It would mean a lot to me."

So Sue, Ted and Steven joined them in one last picture before the babies were too tired to continue. Ember stood leaning against her husband's shoulder, Wyatt in her arms, and a stray ribbon pushed into Wyatt's mouth on his fist. Casey held Will in one strong arm, and Steven stood proud and tall between Ember and Sue, a smile on his face and his rumpled curls just a little askew in the warm wind. Sue was looking down at her son with a proud smile on her face. And Ember looked into the camera, her eyes glittering with the joy that overflowed her heart.

It would be Ember's favorite family photo from the wedding—it brought them all together.

God created a family that day that would settle on the same land where the Harpers had persevered generations before. Sometimes God answered more than one prayer at once, like when He knocked down walls and brought true love to lonely hearts. Or when mothers prayed with all their strength that God would provide for their children when they couldn't do any more…

A family was God's sweetest answer to so many persevering prayers.

* * * * *

If you enjoyed this story, look for
The Lawman's Runaway Bride *and*
The Deputy's Unexpected Family *by Patricia Johns.*

Dear Reader,

If you enjoyed this story about a mother's prayer, why not try some of my other books in my backlist? All of my books are sweet, family friendly and written by the same Christian author.

You can find me at PatriciaJohnsRomance.com, where I write about my upcoming releases and my day-to-day writing life. You can also connect with me on Facebook and Twitter, where I enjoy chatting with my readers. I'd love to see you there!

Patricia

Get 4 FREE REWARDS!

We'll send you 2 FREE Books plus 2 FREE Mystery Gifts.

Love Inspired® books feature contemporary inspirational romances with Christian characters facing the challenges of life and love.

FREE Value Over **$20**

YES! Please send me 2 FREE Love Inspired® Romance novels and my 2 FREE mystery gifts (gifts are worth about $10 retail). After receiving them, if I don't wish to receive any more books, I can return the shipping statement marked "cancel." If I don't cancel, I will receive 6 brand-new novels every month and be billed just $5.24 for the regular-print edition or $5.74 each for the larger-print edition in the U.S., or $5.74 each for the regular-print edition or $6.24 for the larger-print edition in Canada. That's a savings of at least 13% off the cover price. It's quite a bargain! Shipping and handling is just 50¢ per book in the U.S. and 75¢ per book in Canada.* I understand that accepting the 2 free books and gifts places me under no obligation to buy anything. I can always return a shipment and cancel at any time. The free books and gifts are mine to keep no matter what I decide.

Choose one: ☐ Love Inspired® Romance
Regular-Print
(105/305 IDN GMY4)

☐ Love Inspired® Romance
Larger-Print
(122/322 IDN GMY4)

Name (please print)

Address   Apt. #

City   State/Province   Zip/Postal Code

Mail to the **Reader Service:**
IN U.S.A.: P.O. Box 1341, Buffalo, NY 14240-8531
IN CANADA: P.O. Box 603, Fort Erie, Ontario L2A 5X3

Want to try 2 free books from another series? Call 1-800-873-8635 or visit www.ReaderService.com.

---

*Terms and prices subject to change without notice. Prices do not include sales taxes, which will be charged (if applicable) based on your state or country of residence. Canadian residents will be charged applicable taxes. Offer not valid in Quebec. This offer is limited to one order per household. Books received may not be as shown. Not valid for current subscribers to Love Inspired Romance books. All orders subject to approval. Credit or debit balances in a customer's account(s) may be offset by any other outstanding balance owed by or to the customer. Please allow 4 to 6 weeks for delivery. Offer available while quantities last.

Your Privacy—The Reader Service is committed to protecting your privacy. Our Privacy Policy is available online at www.ReaderService.com or upon request from the Reader Service. We make a portion of our mailing list available to reputable third parties that offer products we believe may interest you. If you prefer that we not exchange your name with third parties, or if you wish to clarify or modify your communication preferences, please visit us at www.ReaderService.com/consumerschoice or write to us at Reader Service Preference Service, P.O. Box 9062, Buffalo, NY 14240-9062. Include your complete name and address.

LI19R

SPECIAL EXCERPT FROM

Love Inspired®

After returning to his Amish community after losing his job in the Englisch world, Aaron King isn't sure if he wants to stay. But the more time he spends training a horse with childhood friend Sally Stoltzfus, the more he begins to believe this is exactly where he belongs.

Read on for a sneak preview of
The Promised Amish Bride *by Marta Perry,*
available February 2019 from Love Inspired!

"Komm now, Aaron. I thought you might be ready to keep your promise to me."

"Promise?" He looked at her blankly.

"You can't have forgotten. You promised you'd wait until I grew up and then you'd marry me."

He stared at her, appalled for what seemed like forever until he saw the laughter in her eyes. "Sally Stoltzfus, you've turned into a threat to my sanity. What are you trying to do, scare me to death?"

She gave a gurgle of laughter. "You looked a little bored with the picnic. I thought I'd wake you up."

"Not bored," he said quickly. "Just…trying to find my way. So you don't expect me to marry you. Anything else I can do that's not so permanent?"

"As a matter of fact, there is. I want you to help me train Star."

So that was it. He frowned, trying to think of a way to refuse that wouldn't hurt her feelings.

"You saw what Star is like," she went on without waiting for an answer. "I've got to get him trained, and soon. And everyone knows that you're the best there is with horses."

"I don't think everyone believes any such thing," he retorted. "They don't know me well enough anymore."

She waved that away. "You've been working with horses

while you were gone. And Zeb always says you were born with the gift."

"Onkel Zeb might be a little bit prejudiced," he said, trying to organize his thoughts. There was no real reason he couldn't help her out, except that it seemed like a commitment, and he didn't intend to tie himself anywhere, not now.

"You can't deny that Star needs help, can you?" Her laughing gaze invited him to share her memory of the previous day.

"He needs help all right, but I don't quite see the point. Can't you use the family buggy when you need it?" He suspected that if he didn't come up with a good reason, he'd find himself working with that flighty gelding.

Her face grew serious suddenly. "As long as I do that, I'm depending on someone else. I want to make my own decisions about when and where I'm going. I'd like to be a bit independent, at least in that. I thought you were the one person who might understand."

That hit him right where he lived. He did understand— that was the trouble. He understood too well, and it made him vulnerable where Sally was concerned. He fumbled for words. "I'd like to help. But I don't know how long I'll be here and—"

"That doesn't matter." Seeing her face change was like watching the sun come out. "I'll take whatever time you can spare. Denke, Aaron. I'm wonderful glad."

He started to say that his words hadn't been a yes, but before he could, Sally had grabbed his hand and every thought flew right out of his head.

It was just like her catching hold of Onkel Zeb's arm, he tried to tell himself. But it didn't work. When she touched him, something seemed to light between them like a spark arcing from one terminal to another. He felt it right down to his toes, and he knew in that instant that he was in trouble.

Don't miss
The Promised Amish Bride *by Marta Perry,*
available February 2019 wherever
Love Inspired® books and ebooks are sold.

www.LoveInspired.com

Looking for inspiration in tales
of hope, faith and heartfelt romance?

Check out **Love Inspired**® and
Love Inspired® Suspense books!

New books available every month!

CONNECT WITH US AT:

Facebook.com/groups/HarlequinConnection

Facebook.com/HarlequinBooks

Twitter.com/HarlequinBooks

Instagram.com/HarlequinBooks

Pinterest.com/HarlequinBooks

ReaderService.com

Inspirational Romance to Warm Your Heart and Soul

Join our social communities to connect with other readers who share your love!

Sign up for the Love Inspired newsletter at **www.LoveInspired.com** to be the first to find out about upcoming titles, special promotions and exclusive content.

CONNECT WITH US AT:

Facebook.com/groups/HarlequinConnection

 Facebook.com/LoveInspiredBooks

 Twitter.com/LoveInspiredBks

LISOCIAL2018

e book you!

Earn points on your purchase of new Harlequin books from participating retailers.

Turn your points into **FREE BOOKS** of your choice!

Join for FREE today at
www.HarlequinMyRewards.com.

Harlequin My Rewards is a free program (no fees) without any commitments or obligations.

MYR18